HITMEN I HAVE KNOWN

HITMEN I HAVE KNOWN

Bill James

This first world edition published 2019
in Great Britain and the USA by
SEVERN HOUSE PUBLISHERS LTD of
Eardley House, 4 Uxbridge Street, London W8 7SY.
Trade paperback edition first published
in Great Britain and the USA 2019 by
SEVERN HOUSE PUBLISHERS LTD.

British Library Cataloguing in Publication Data
A CIP catalogue record for this title is available from the British Library.

ISBN-13: 978-0-7278-8866-2 (cased)
ISBN-13: 978-1-84751-990-0 (trade paper)
ISBN-13: 978-1-4483-0202-4 (e-book)

Typeset by Palimpsest Book Production Ltd.,
Falkirk, Stirlingshire, Scotland.

ONE

Iles said: 'Assistant chief constable (Operations)', except that, as always, he loaded several more 's' sounds front and middle to 'assistant' so that it came out as 'assssissstant', fizzing with hate and disgust for his own title and job. Iles *was* the assistant chief constable (Operations). This he could not deny or alter, to date at least. Instead, he'd invented a contemptuous, brush-off style for naming his rank.

The bumper quantity of these s's didn't signal dangerous aggression, like the hiss of a snake or cornered alley cat, but echoed their slimy use, double or single, in words like 'subservient', 'slavish', 'subordinate', 'servile'.

'Assssissstant chief constable (Operations),' Iles said. 'What does it mean? At root, what does it mean?' Iles freighted in bags of modest puzzlement to his tone.

'That's certainly a point, sir,' Harpur suggested.

'Above an "assssissstant" chief constable there obviously has to be a topmost officer, a chief constable, for the assssissstant chief constable to be assssissstant to. Right?' Iles said. 'This figure – the chief – has been appointed because he or she is deemed to have great personal, indeed unique, qualities of leadership, isn't he or she?'

'Few would deny this.'

'Which fucking "few"?'

'Leadership is quite a topic,' Harpur replied.

'The chief, he or she, is different from all his or her colleagues. It's why he or she *is* chief. So, how can one of those colleagues, from whom the chief is different, help – assssissst – him or her to become even more different from and better than the person trying to help – assssissst – him or her with qualities which the assssissstant supposedly hasn't got or he or she would be not just an assssissstant?'

Once in a while, often unexpectedly, Iles liked to analyse his situation as an assistant in what seemed to Harpur this kind of thorough, merciless, half-barmy fashion. He would seem dogged by unanswerable questions.

Harpur said: 'My mother often remarks without the least prompting that life's full of conundrums.'

'Does she, Harpur?'

'Oh, yes.'

'Occasionally, or even more often than that, they mean well,' Iles said.

'Who?'

'Mothers.'

'Comments,' Harpur said. 'These are what she likes to make, sometimes on quite big problems. Show her a problem and most likely she'll comment on it, one way or the other, full blast without prejudice.'

'Which kind?'

'Which kind of what, sir?'

'Prejudice. Which kind of prejudice is it without?'

'I don't mind, regardless,' Harpur said.

'Cardboard,' Iles replied.

'In what sense, sir?'

'My rank, my post, Colin,' Iles said. 'No substance. Flimsy. What can it do for me when I am badgered by crisis, encircled by enemies? Answer? Little, or less. In fact, one could say that it's on account of this very rank and position that I'm threatened now – so vindictively threatened now. Have you heard, Col, there might be some sort of television thing about it?'

They were talking in Harpur's room at headquarters. Iles would sometimes look in if he was feeling low or enraged or troubled by pubic lice. Because he might have had the room bugged, Harpur was always careful about what he said during these visits. He did frequent searches for any listening mics, but had found nothing. Iles was clever, though. There were numerous pieces of electronic and other equipment in the room and he might have found a way of concealing something tiny and super-efficient.

Of course, the bug, if it was there, would be meant mainly to record conversations Harpur had with others, not with Iles. There'd be no obvious point in recording talk between Harpur and him because Iles had taken part in the talk and knew what was said. In that alert, hugely untrusting, creative mode of his, though, Iles might want to replay and re-replay the chat, and search for hidden, unconscious give-aways in the word order, volume – or lack of it – and timbre of what Harpur said.

Harpur had found that the best way to counter this was extreme terseness or its opposite: rambling, verbose, trite, massively irrelevant digressions, such as Harpur's mention of his mother just now. He was a detective chief super-intendent, head of Iles's staff, and knew the assistant chief constantly feared Harpur or someone else – but especially Harpur – might get ahead of him in knowledge of one or more of the cases they handled. Iles believed important infor-mation was often held back from him. Harpur knew this to be very shrewd and very reasonable in Iles, because he did at times hold back important information, particularly infor-mation that was not only important but exceptionally important. Good policing demanded subtlety and constant self-protection. And so the search for bugs, the wise rationing of disclosures, and the delivery by Harpur of truisms, clichés and general windbaggery.

The assistant chief was sitting on one of the two easy chairs in Harpur's room. He was slim bordering on thin, mid-height, though exceptionally proud of his legs, his very blue eyes brilliantly alight with egomania and insolence. If they were going to get an actor to play him under a disguised name in this 'television thing' he'd spoken about, the eyes would be very hard to mimic. He was wearing his grey hair quite long at present after a spell *en brosse*, copied from Jean Gabin, the French actor, in old films on The Movie Channel. Iles must have tired of that. There was a kind of refinement to his face, a radiantly dodgy kind. He had his chin slightly lowered so as to cut off Harpur's sight of the ACC's Adam's apple, which he regarded as unmatched for ugliness among the Adam's apples of the world, and a monstrous, undeserved blight. There were rumours that Iles had made inquiries about cosmetic surgery to rid him of this blot but hadn't proceeded with it so far. Iles had what Harpur regarded as a kind of obsession about Adam's apples. He used to mock a previous chief's because it was too bulky and angular. But Harpur thought this was only an attempt by Iles to switch people's attention from his.

Iles said: 'They want to prove I murdered two villains who'd dodged a murder conviction a while ago, one a garrotting with rope and a bit of broken broom handle inserted between the two strands for tightening through a seven- or eight-minute period, the rope fairly thin so it can bite into the neck, but, obviously, strong enough to sustain the unyielding, essential pressure.'

'Yes,' Harpur replied.

'Yes?'

'Yes.'

'What the hell are you getting at, Harpur?'

'Getting at in which respect, sir?'

'The "Yes". Its category.'

'Category?'

'Are you saying to me, "Yes, you did see off two villains a while ago"?'

'My daughters tell me it's popular in *The Godfather,* a quite well-known film about gangsters,' Harpur replied.

'What is?'

'Garrotting.'

'Your daughters are children. Why would they discuss something so distasteful?'

'These films come up on The Movie Channel, like the Gabin pics, or there are DVDs,' Harpur said.

'As a matter of fact, some countries used garrotting as their method of state execution,' Iles replied.

'It's reasonably easy to organize. A scaffold not needed.'

'Not at all,' Iles said.

'Most probably you've given it some thought, sir, over the years when it came up in cases.'

'Given what some thought?'

'Garrotting,' Harpur said.

'We're talking about one garrotted, one shot, aren't we? They're going to do some sort of telly documentary on it.'

'But obviously they won't be able to say you did them, sir. That would be stark libel. Plus, another reason, they're not going to say it because, of course, it can't be true,' Harpur said.

'Can't be?' Iles replied. 'You're an assistant chief constable. Officers of that rank don't go around garrotting people, no matter how much those people fooled the courts and deserved garrotting and/or getting shot. But the TV boys and girls like a good tale, don't they, sir? It would be quite a thing for them to show someone of such high position and esteem as an ACC – though an ACC with a telly-script fend-off name and nature – performing that sort of neck job, plus another killing.'

'That's why I said my title and rank are a bugbear,' Iles explained. 'They invite loathing and malice and doctoring of the truth.' He switched to a kindly, sweet lilt. 'But fret not, Col. With those clothes and Palookaville haircut, you'll never reach this rank and all its hazards yourself and I congratulate you on that.'

'Thank you, sir.'

TWO

Harpur had a call from Jack Lamb, the art dealer and world-quality informant. Although he undoubtedly *was* world-quality, the world got no tip-offs of any quality at all from him. Harpur did. Only Harpur did. Jack spoke secrets to nobody else. This defied the rules. These were very specific, and very purposeful. They lay down that an informant did not belong to any individual officer but to the whole detective force. Not Jack. The arrangement was one to one, strictly one to one: Lamb to Harpur, Harpur to Lamb. Harpur's daughters had some idea of what went on and the older one, Hazel, had asked, 'Is that why you have such big, flappy ears, Dad, so he can whisper sweet somethings confidentially into them?'

In tune with this long-term understanding between him and Lamb, Harpur had decided a good while ago that it would be stupidly officious and tactless to ask ticklish questions about the legality or not of Jack's business. Most probably parts of it were absolutely legit and Harpur made do with that. He didn't know much about art but he knew what he liked, and what he liked was for Jack to be accessible and ready with his kind of special revelations, not in the clink.

This kind of concealed, illicit, personal connection between a successful officer and his/her informant was probably not unique. Harpur didn't feel certain about this because secrecy had to stay absolute. Harpur knew that Lamb would have refused to operate in any other way. He'd most likely regard a relationship with the entire Criminal Investigation Department as sluttish. Sensitive information had a value and, like everything else in the market, its value increased with scarcity. And so Jack made his information not just scarce but entirely absent for everyone except Harpur.

This didn't mean Harpur slipped him big payments or any payments at all, but guaranteed a friendly failure by Harpur to not question where some of the pics and sculpts Jack traded with came from, and where they went, but especially not where they came from. Villains used fine art to launder drugs money, protection money, fraud money, general racket money. It would probably surprise great painters that their works could be evaluated in terms of snorts. Crooks bought pictures and sculptures, held them for a while then put them up for apparently innocent re-sale. Harpur followed a 'Don't ask' policy. This was close to complicity. He knew it and for now put up with the conditions. These were complex and not always very wholesome.

Lamb wanted a meeting. Jack would use the phone to name a place and time but not for anything longer. Informants risked their safety and tried to keep that risk small. He considered phones, landline or mobile, as 'spewers', liable to be overheard throwing up classified facts.

Harpur and Lamb varied their rendezvous locations, and had a code name for each. Lately, they'd added a new one to their three rotating regulars because . . . because they had become regular and that worried Jack. Perhaps someone would notice a pattern, and that someone might not be a helpful someone. Unhelpful someones abounded. The three meeting spots were:

(a) An old wartime concrete defence post on the foreshore, still waiting for enemy landing craft;

(b) A side-street laundrette where each would arrive with a bag of washing and talk quietly while watching through the glass panels their stuff slither and plunge and sidle;

(c) Another wartime relic – hillside remains of the anti-aircraft gun emplacements built to knock down raiding Heinkels and Dorniers in the 1940s.

Now, they had a (d): the privately run rubbish and recycling site on the almost rural western edge of the city. In the evenings it was closed and they could park alongside each other at its gates. Harpur wondered whether they might look like a couple of 'doggers', together for random, anonymous car sex, but they'd chance it. A notice fixed to the gates' iron struts said that 78 per cent of the items dumped there in the previous three months had been successfully recycled as metal, wooden and horticultural material. Harpur thought that perhaps Jack wanted some of this positive atmosphere to reach their meetings when he suggested the new venue. Many regarded informing as deeply and unambiguously odious. A link to something good and constructive such as recycling might help correct this.

Very occasionally, Harpur already knew from another source, or other sources, the information Jack brought him, though he would never let Lamb realize this. It would damage his pride. He had to be sheltered and cherished. This was one of the unspoken conditions of their unwritten, unpermitted, undisclosed contract. Harpur wanted it undiscovered, unendangered and unterminated.

They were in the front seats of Jack's crimson Lexus. He had on what Harpur guessed to be the striped uniform of the Vatican Swiss Guard: blue, red, orange, yellow, but with a British commando green beret. Jack liked military surplus clothes, though he didn't care about accuracy. Harpur thought it a weird taste for someone so keen on security and concealment. But Jack was 6 foot 5 inches and more than 250 pounds, so possibly he didn't really believe he could ever go unnoticed, anyway.

Tonight felt to Harpur like one of those instances when he'd be told something he didn't need to be told. Harpur couldn't have explained why, or not very clearly. He feared it might be vanity. Was he coming to believe he'd been at this game for so long that he probably knew now by gifted instinct everything he ought to know? First step towards megalomaniac lunacy?

Jack said, chattily enough, 'There seem to be a lot of investigations at present of what are called "historic" offences, don't you think, Colin? Mainly sexual, but other kinds, too, men – it's always men – men charged with crimes committed – allegedly committed – years ago, and stars many of them?'

Harpur thought he knew what might be coming and went chewy and very evasive, what Harpur's daughters called his 'know-all plonking' voice. Although he prized the kind of insights Lamb often brought him, he didn't like hearing Jack's splendid talents applied to private, internal police matters. Harpur did a bit of a now-hear-this chunter. 'There've always been cases that were unresolved at the time, but then, much later, a new piece of evidence shows up and clinches everything,' he said. 'DNA might not have been available originally, but now it can give the truth. Many examples. The murderer of a prostitute in Wales was caught like that, ages after the killing – and ages after wrongful conviction of several men for her death. Also, there was a powerful campaign led by very loud, distinguished people to prove James Hanratty innocent of murder and rape, but DNA eventually showed he was guilty of both when hanged.'

'Iles,' Jack replied.

As replies went, Harpur didn't like this one very much, but there it was and had better be dealt with. He trundled on with his attempt at diversion. 'Or a new witness might decide to bring something absolutely crucial to what had been an unbustable mystery. These days, there's so-called "double jeopardy".' Previously, no one could be tried for the same crime twice. Now, though, Jack, there's jeopardy – the first trial – but also the chance of another one – another helping of hazard in court, a second jeopardy. The past, the historic, became much more reachable and forced the change in the law.'

'Garrotting is a topic that figures,' Jack Lamb replied.

'Plus, of course, the Stephen Lawrence case,' Harpur said. 'A black teenager was stabbed to death in London and a group of white youths was accused but found not guilty of the killing. Then, though, two were retried and jailed because of new scientific evidence. History, yes, but history that has come alive.'

Lamb said: 'It's not only Mr Iles I wanted to talk about; this affects you as well, Colin. That's what troubles me. Mr Iles is important, definitely, but I considered it a prime duty to look after you. I felt I should get in touch with a warning. There's two sides to these developments: first, the situation itself; second, TV might want to make something of it.'

'Always glad to hear from you, Jack,' Harpur replied.

'Oh, you talk breezy, but this is serious. If I see you're at risk I have to act, haven't I? The whole beautiful, time-shaped structure is threatened.'

'Structure?'

'This.'

'What?'

'Meetings like tonight's. Or at the other places. A system. A structure. We've built it.'

'I like the idea, Jack – a structure.'

'Of course you do. You belong to one – another one: the police. There's the chief, then Mr Iles, then you. That's a structure. But we have our own.'

Harpur had wondered sometimes whether Jack's fondness for military gear showed a longing to be part of some platoon or squadron or flotilla, with its own clan solidarity and discipline – its structure, maybe. The Swiss Guards and British commandos would have their strictly organized lives and so would the Pope and priests whom the guards had in their care: structure upon structure.

'I see,' Harpur said.

'That structure – ours – is threatened,' Jack said.

'In which respect?'

'Gravely.'

'Where does it come from – the threat?'

'Our happy cooperation might have to end.'

'How do you know this, Jack? Who's been talking to you?'

Naturally, no informant would answer that breed of question, or, at least, not with the truth. To ask it, though, was one of those formalities from Harpur's training that sometimes surfaced, a sort of automatic twitch.

'There's movement, Col.'

'In which respect?'

'That's what I mean about past cases,' Lamb said. 'Revived interest in them. It's dangerous. It's modish. It helps those interested feel vigilant and nobly persistent. Television adores the topic. Producers see a potential programme in the way that garrotting and non-garrotting deaths have been investigated, or not.'

They'd arrived at about the same time and had both driven front-on to the gates and shut off their lights. Then Harpur had joined Jack in his car. Now, Harpur heard a faint, gentle but persistent noise, a sort of rustling or shuffling, from nearby, and flicked the Lexus main beam on briefly. A couple of hundred rats were busying about between the dump bins and junked fridges. They took no notice of the lights. But they'd obviously been scared by the noise of two car engines when Lamb and Harpur turned up together, and had gone out of sight. They'd come back now.

Harpur thought they must have some system, some team structure – Jack's word – to their activity. He couldn't work it out, though. Jill, his other daughter, had told him not long ago that her biology teacher mentioned a strange book about rats. It described how a zoologist who'd been studying their ways became so impressed by their organizing and social skills that he'd decided to join them and left papers explaining why and how. This was a made-up story, though. Harpur had thought it a bit far-fetched, but what he saw now made him wonder. Rats were said to leave a sinking ship. They sensed disaster before the crew did. Superior intelligence?

How would the rats feel about this scholar wishing to ratify himself by, so to speak, *ratifying* himself? Harpur opened the door of the car and stepped out in what he hoped was a courteous, unaggressive style. The rats offered no welcome but withdrew again for cover among the bins and kitchen equipment. It was an urgent but orderly retreat. Harpur got back into the Lexus and turned the lights off. Before he shut the door he heard their pitter-patter returning. Smart.

Lamb ignored the break in their talk. 'You'll know the phrase "rough justice", Colin.'

'It contradicts itself.'

'Perhaps.'

'It means justice without the essentials of justice such as a fair examination of all the facts, and therefore isn't justice at all. It's the lynch mob.'

'Maybe proper justice has failed,' Lamb said. 'And now and then it does – or someone believes it has, because it didn't offer the right result.'

'The desired result.'

'I'm talking about the garrotting and so on, aren't I, Colin?'

'Are you?'

'How do we regard those deaths, Colin? Think: In some countries, State executions are, or were, by garrotting,' Lamb said.

'Yes, I've heard that.'

'Could I ask where you heard it?' Lamb said.

'Oh, it would be in conversation, I expect.'

'Yes, I expect,' Lamb said. 'If you heard it how else could that have happened?'

'Where or when I don't recall,' Harpur said.

'But do you recall who with?'

'Difficult.'

'It must be an enthusiastic fan of garrotting,' Lamb said.

'That should certainly reduce the number of possibles,' Harpur replied.

'And someone who most likely believes in garrotting as one method of personal execution, if the law has failed to punish flagrant villainy. This is the sort of controversial situation that the TV people will love to exploit in a slightly tarted-up, semi-fictionalized documentary.'

Someone pulled open a rear door of the Lexus and climbed in. It was possibly a practised movement, smooth, athletic and swift, adaptable for any make of four-door car; no violent, raiding tug at the door but gentle, and easy-going, as though they're entitled to enter. The approach to the car must have been skilled and well-angled. Harpur had seen nothing. Lamb wouldn't have central locking on while the Lexus was occupied, so no trouble about entry.

Harpur and Jack both turned. There was a little, intermittent light when a three-quarters moon came out from behind clouds. 'Hello! and felicitations! Are you boys looking for some veritable, indiscriminate closeness?' the man said. He'd be mid-fifties, Harpur thought, with a nicely cut suede jacket, vermilion T-shirt, scrumpy-enhanced breath, voice light and upbeat, acquainted with ejaculations. He was white with a thin, bony face and small, fair moustache; the kind of face Harpur had often seen under a courtroom wig. He closed the door behind him. It made a hearty, heavy-duty, limo-category click. The Lexus felt homely.

'I like them big,' the man said, 'and you two are, in fact, that, one enormous. Not perfect light, but I can tell you're in a sensational outfit, Mr Heavyweight behind the wheel. Don't tell me. Swiss Guard? Not the hat, of course – John Wayne green beret. To dress like that is use of colour as a fine, respectful compliment to our very amiable, bracing pursuits. Of course, I saw your joyously vivid signal just now, the flashed headlights. It really beckoned. Thank you, oh, thank you. Those beams, so powerful, so far-reaching, yet also reaching *me*, in my car not far off and, like you, awaiting high-jinks. Oh, yes, jinks very much at the high end of the jinks agenda. In which regard, I hurried here, oh, hurried, hurried, like compelled, like magnetized, knowing that your rear seat was aching with welcome and that I need not fear rejection or brutality, other, of course, than tasty, charmingly stimulating brutality.

'My name's Zachary but Zed will do. Did you see the rats, their pelts so made-to-measure, so silvery in the beams, their eyes roguish, no resentment at the human intrusion? What a gorgeous backdrop to our explorations! Thrilling! Threesomes – don't you adore them, so much more range than just two or self-catering? Do you like silence during things or lots of worldly, explicit wordage and rousing squeaks? You're the Lexus sex-us host and set the terms. I acknowledge that without demur. I keep demurs to an absolute minimum these days.'

'We're leaving now, Zed,' Harpur replied. 'Disembark please. The rats won't attack. I've shown them we're nicely behaved and harmless.'

'Oh?'

'Perhaps on another occasion,' Jack replied. 'This chic pleasure garden is on our map now.'

'I might not be available. There are uncompromising calls upon my time,' Zed said.

'Same here,' Harpur said.

'I'm very into *carpe diem*,' Zed said.

'It suits you,' Harpur replied.

'That's "seize the day", of course, or more likely night,' Zed said.

Lamb said, '*Scarper diem*, OK?'

Zed began to weep, perhaps emotionally hurt and frustrated by this clumsy harshness from Jack. The sobs were profound and noisy, seeming to come from a good stand-by store sub-chest, like someone doing grief at a screen test. He put a hand

on each side of his face and banged his forehead down repeatedly and rhythmically on the back of Jack's seat. The sound
of this hammering plus the quality sobs suggested that things
had ceased to be OK in the Lexus: a possible happy evening had
turned out very poorly. Did the Swiss Guard uniform aggra-
vate things? A unit that took care of the Vatican should surely
know about holy kindness and humane behaviour. Maybe Zed
expected that sort of response. Lamb's actual response,
though, was the reverse of this, and as a result super-shocking
and painful.

Harpur felt a lot of sympathy for this stranger, though did
not weep himself. He stepped out of the Lexus again and
went around to a rear door and helped him down. The rats
stayed out of sight. Harpur walked with the man back to his
Subaru. 'Never shall I approach a parked Lexus again, no
matter how many are in it – one, two or even more,' he said,
'and no matter if I am summoned and summoned repeatedly
by headlights.'

'I don't think it's reasonable or fair to blame all Lexuses,'
Harpur replied.

'It's my nature.'

'What is?'

'Genres. The Lexus is a genre, yes?'

'It's a make.'

'If one member of a genre rejects me it is as though *all*
members of that genre reject me.' He was no longer sobbing,
though his voice remained shaky. 'My body will not allow me
to engage with any vehicle of that specific breed. It would be
a betrayal, a descent into ignoble catch-as-catch-can.'

Harpur left him at the Subaru. As he walked back to his
car and the Lexus he thought some more about the development over the millennia of rats' intelligence. It enabled them
now to order their lives so slickly: to have no fear of main-
beam headlights, but to watch out for someone taking a walk
very near their ground. He did feel some envy. In comparison,
his life seemed over-complex. He had to deal with rumour;
with a Subaru hysteric; with history, disputed history, dangerous
history – dangerous to Iles and to himself; with possible TV
half-truths; with justice as against so-called 'rough justice',

and with the safety of someone who should be able to secure his own safety, and had done that so far, but might in new conditions fail: Iles. The Lexus moved off before Harpur reached the two vehicles. Jack didn't wave. He looked crusty and must be feeling resentful and embarrassed. He'd picked this dump as a rendezvous point and it was clear now that it wouldn't really do. The rats might be interesting, but there was also Zed, and possibly other doggers waiting out of sight. Discreet it wasn't.

Harpur could understand Jack's disappointment and forgive a bit of rudeness. But Zed might feel otherwise. Jack had been crudely harsh to him with that dud joke: '*Scarper diem*, OK?' Harpur had tried to dish out comfort and end the volcanic blubbering, but Zed stayed badly upset. His sad, cranky embargo on all Lexus cars came from a mind not working too well. And if he saw Jack drive off, like in a bitter rage, rejecting the whole scene and those involved in it tonight, this would injure Zed even more.

Harpur decided it would be heartless to leave Zed in that state. He turned and went back to the Subaru. He'd decided he must bring Zed another slice of consolation – make up, if he could, for Jack's ugly surliness. The rat civilization could certainly teach him plenty.

Zed was behind the wheel of the Subaru as Harpur had left him a few minutes ago. He had been alone in the car then. But alongside him in the passenger seat now was a man of about his own age, grey moustached and bearded, in a denim jacket with a silver and blue cravat on a white shirt. Zed looked totally recovered and splendidly happy, not sobbing, and as though he wouldn't actually know *how* to sob or what a sob was.

The man in the passenger seat had evidently watched Harpur approach. Urgently he rolled the side window down and called out in a shrill, panicky voice, 'No room, no room.' Then he bent forward to get a better look at Harpur through the windscreen. There were some minutes of moonlight. 'Oh,' he said. 'Cor!'

'What?' Zed said.

The man spoke to Harpur. 'Aren't you that dick?'

'Which?' Zed said.

'Which what?' the man said.

'Dick,' Zed said. 'You need to be specific about something like that.'

'On TV local news now and then about crimes. Police. Big-time cop detective,' the man replied.

'Really?' Zed said.

'Plain clothes,' the man said.

'His partner has on a very vivid and very becoming costume,' Zed replied. 'This I can vouch for.'

'Due to be inquired into,' the man said.

'Who?' Zed said.

'The top-spot detective,' the man said. 'He's powerful, but did he use that power right?'

'Did he?' Zed said.

'Why there's an inquiry,' the man said.

'Historic. To do with two murders a while ago. A couple of crooks. Did they get investigated properly? Or was it a cover-up to protect another top cop – even more top, in fact. Revenge killings? Illegal punishments? An outside team will do some very serious, modish probing. That's the word around.'

'Around where?' Harpur said.

'Around. For instance, in the business community. There's a commercial angle to something like this. People worry. People discuss. It's in the air. Implications. Long-term shifts.'

Zed now bent forward, bent forward further than the passenger-seat man so as to speak to Harpur direct across him. 'Although I've only just met Stanley I can tell he will be a triumph of mixed impulses and jolly skills. But I can tell, too, that he's not into threesomes or more, I'm afraid,' Zed said. 'Sorry.'

'No room, no room,' Stanley shrieked, closing the window.

THREE

Harpur drove home to Arthur Street. He felt disturbed. He would have liked someone with whom he could talk over these hints, and more than hints, that he heard lately about a possible – probable? certain? – cold-case inquiry into the deaths of those two flagrant, acquitted villains who were either shot or garrotted. When Jack Lamb brought you information – at a rubbish dump or anywhere else – you'd better believe it, especially if Iles had told you approximately the same.

The someone he would most like to talk to about it was Denise, his undergraduate, frequently live-in girlfriend. She had a tidy, unflinching brain, which could take a problem and methodically shred it into very manageable bits, then reassemble them and produce a convincing answer. She said she'd learned this technique from the French philosophers she was reading at university, known as *'cassez pour construire'* – 'break open to create'. Harpur, though, thought it a flair she was born with. The French philosophers might have given it a polish, that was all.

But, regardless of where it came from, Harpur couldn't let her loose on these particular anxieties. Couldn't? He was scared to. This made him ashamed, but not ashamed enough to tell her. She might separate out all his worries in that clever way of hers, then put them back together but with the kind of answer he definitely did not want. He'd begun to ask himself whether he had been slack and deliberately dozy in dealing with the murder of those two villains because . . . well, because they were villains and ought to expect something like that; and . . . and . . . and because of the unthinkable: that Iles, as assistant chief constable (Operations), had somehow been involved in those hastened deaths.

Denise didn't believe anything was unthinkable. Perhaps the French philosophers taught her this. Apparently one of them had said, 'I think therefore I am,' but she reshaped it to 'I am, therefore I think' – and think about anything I fancy. If he took his troubles to her she'd give them a close eyeballing and might come to suspect there really had been some dozy slackness, because she would see a reason for it – a lawless, wrong, lynch-mob-type reason, but still a reason. Harpur feared that if she began to think like this it would do her opinion of him damage. That's what made him nervous. He needed her absolute, unwavering approval and love.

Denise was twenty and at university, Harpur thirty-seven, a widower with two teenage daughters. This wasn't a vast and unbridgeable difference, but it made Harpur feel very lucky and very vulnerable. He would like to stay lucky. His children adored Denise and they wanted him to stay lucky, too, so they wouldn't lose her.

Perhaps tonight, when he got back from the Lamb meeting and they'd had supper, she sensed that he had a private fret or two. She didn't quiz him about it then, though; she had her own way of dealing with it. In bed she drew back the duvet and went over him toe to temple with her mouth in something more than a kiss but less than a suck – a sort of gentle brushing of her lips, moving eventually up to *his* mouth and lips, and this was a true kiss, true kisses. He didn't mind the smell of Marlboros on her breath, as long as the breath was hers, and as long as he was the only man getting it. Almost everything about Denise delighted him. It had been a long time since Harpur had had any other woman's ciggie smoke in his face.

He didn't try to remember when or whose now, though. He already suffered that shame and guilt for hiding his possible rough news. He wouldn't add to these. Denise played in the college lacrosse team and she mounted him now in a swift, powerfully athletic swivel that probably owed a bit to sports training. Harpur believed though it owed more to her project to give him, and get for herself, a right beautiful and cheery fuck.

FOUR

Ralph Ember – sometimes called 'Panicking Ralph' or 'Panicking Ralphy', but not to his face – owned a popular drinking club, The Monty, at 11 Shield Terrace in the southeast of the city, and he heard quite a lot of rumour and gossip from members there. Most of this rumour and gossip turned out to be *only* rumour and gossip, like rumour and gossip anywhere, and time killed it off, generally, quite soon. But lately there'd seemed something much more enduring and consistent in this talk. It centred on one person: assistant chief constable (Operations) Desmond Iles.

Ember always tried to be moderate and measured in how he spoke, so he never actually *said* he detested Iles. He detested Iles, though. If arrogance was a feasible characteristic for arseholes, Ralph reckoned Iles was an arrogant arsehole. Some nights the assistant chief constable (Operations) would come to The Monty in uniform, silver braided cap on, generally accompanied by his sidekick in plain clothes, Detective Chief Superintendent Colin Harpur. Between them, they could turn the atmosphere of the club more or less instantly sepulchral. The pair probably knew what good fellowship was but enjoyed kicking it to death at The Monty.

Some people always left immediately after those two appeared at the club, not even bothering to finish their drinks or conversations. Iles might yodel genuinely heartfelt farewells after them – 'pederasts', 'knicker-sniffers', 'Adam's apples', 'charity workers', 'coprophiliacs', 'fraudsters', 'poets', 'muggers' – and would stare about at the others who remained in the bar, Iles grinning like an open wound, as though they all ought to be in jail and soon would be following one of his operations.

Ralph thought Iles loved creating this chill in The Monty. Ember had heard of a bar in Stockholm where everything was made of ice. Most likely, Iles regarded it as a competitor.

Officially, he and Harpur came to check the club still met its licence conditions, but Ralph reckoned they were actually there only to mess him about. He liked to imagine while fixing their drinks that if he asked Iles, 'What's your poison, sir?' the assistant chief constable (Operations) would reply, 'I am.'

A dream. Ralph had to put up with the real Iles, three dimensional – and thank God not more than three – fiendish, and effortlessly clever. Ember naturally wanted to discover, if he could, whatever there was to know about him so he could shape up his hit-backs.

In a strange and yet very understandable, even logical, way, it was on a festival night at The Monty that Ralph heard what might be the start of something deep and serious about Iles. Before this, Ralph had picked up fragments only. He might catch a mention of the name – 'Ralph', 'Ralphy', 'Ember', 'Panicking', – when two or three people in the club were chatting, plus a few other words, but no real meaningful information. What he *had* noticed, though, tonight, was the constant flavour of the remarks: giggly, relaxed, unafraid, not normally the mode when someone spoke about Iles.

The more usual tone would be bewilderment and escalating dread. Ralph Ember hoped and bravely believed that one day he would see no more of the menace Iles invariably brought with him to the Monty in its present state.

Those words – 'in its present state' – were crucial, and Ralph had golden ambitions for The Monty and aimed to make it as distinguished, influential and refined as, say, The Athenaeum or The Carlton clubs in London.

He knew this would not happen speedily. Until then, The Monty remained a fondly esteemed local meeting spot, the natural, friendly, welcoming venue for bail or acquittal celebrations – especially acquittals that were brilliantly against the odds – wedding receptions, end-of-jail-term parties, raves, christening sprees, victory piss-ups after turf fights, post-funeral wind-downs, tribute evenings on important anniversaries, witness statement withdrawals, parole successes.

There were certain cast-iron restrictions. Pimping and drugs pushing on Monty premises Ralph absolutely banned. These could bring bitter, violent trouble. Ralph had seen it happen in other clubs. The drop in reputation might be serious and long-lasting. He believed commercial pussy simply as commercial pussy could sometimes produce problems, but commercial pussy on coke meant unstinting noisy peril, broken glass, blood-stained décor, carpets and pool tables, torn garments and flying spit. Very injurious chuck-outs had occasionally been necessary, including a dislocated shoulder and short-term concussion.

He would admit that people living in Shield Terrace might feel uneasy about some of the scrapping, screams and blasphemies near the club, but he thought that, once he'd turned The Monty into a brilliant social and intellectual hub, Shield Terrace would become wonderfully smart, fashionable and vibrant with a sparkling increase in the value of their properties. Ralph himself lived outside the city at Low Pastures near Apsley's farm, a lovely converted manor house with wide grounds, but he could still sympathize with what the residents of Shield Terrace felt.

The Monty festive date that helped readjust Ralph's view of Iles was Bastille Day. Ralph counted himself a terrific admirer of France and the French. He loved the way they baked twice a day so their bread was always fresh. Each 14 July he ran a colourful shindig at The Monty – tricolour flags, bunting, balloons, photographs of Edith Piaf, Charles de Gaulle, Brigitte Bardot, Maurice Chevalier, Jean Gabin and Napoleon – to commemorate the start of the Revolution in 1789, when citizens stormed the Bastille and freed prisoners locked up by a corrupt regime. The period fascinated Ralph. Central to it was a vicious, ruthlessly scheming politician, Robespierre, responsible for a time of great barbarity in France called 'The Terror', and who seemed to Ralph like an early, test-run version of Iles. Most probably Iles would agree.

Ralph had begun a degree course for mature students in one of the local universities – suspended at present because of intense and welcome business demands, especially coke – and in the Foundation Year had been asked to write about the effects of the Revolution. He had excelled at that. Now, he liked to act out those basic aims and demands of the French Revolution: liberty, equality, fraternity.

On the Bastille nights at the club he mingled more with the members than usual. Once in a while he was prepared to think of The Monty customers as equal to himself, or close, though he would never let this become an untidy habit. And, alarmingly, it was because he'd taken the liberty to come out from behind the bar for a bit of fraternity that he heard more about Iles.

In honour of the triumphant attack on the Bastille, Monty drinks were free until one a.m. 'Ralph! Pray join us,' Tim ('Tasteful') Barry-Longville said. Tasteful and his mother were on Cointreau. Ralph brought a bottle of that and one of Kressmann Armagnac and a glass for himself. He sat down at their table. Tasteful was some sort of executive at the local evening paper, *The Scene*. He always wore a very dark double-breasted suit, white shirt and subdued tie when he came to the club. Ralph thought he might be able to let him join the new Monty when it was created. Ralph would want and need such nicely dressed members with decent jobs. Tasteful's mother, Mavis, was in a long, light ochre and silver summer dress with a pearl necklace.

'I've always loved that black label of the Kressmann brew,' she said. 'So understated. So in keeping with the smooth, sugarless content.'

'True,' Ralph said.

'Your teeth – a testimony to the drink's beneficence.'

'I think so,' Ralph replied.

'These are teeth that by their bites bring distinction to what is being eaten. It's a charming reciprocity,' she replied.

'Thank you,' Ralph said.

'We've been discussing the past,' Mavis said.

'Ah, yes,' Ralph said.

'Not an inert, abandoned past,' she said.

'No,' Tasteful said. 'I'd mentioned garrotting. Such a picturesque method of snuffing out someone, the ligature so apparently harmless until actually applied, and then the useless, frantic struggles of the recipient.'

'This is a French occasion, so I tend to think of French connections, as it were,' Mavis replied. 'Talking of the past, perhaps you'll recall that de Musset poem, Ralph.'

'Ah,' Ralph said.

'This is not to do with the garrotting and so on, I think, is it, Mother?' Tasteful asked.

'Let me see now – how does it go? Yes.' She got some plaintiveness into her voice: "*Regrettez-vous le temps où le ciel sur la terre / Marchait et respirait dans un peuple de dieux?*" That's one view of the past, isn't it? The poet asks, don't we regret not being around when the classical gods were supposedly running their lives, here below on earth? I think I do sort of regret it, though I wouldn't want to get shagged by a swan, like Leda – all that wing-flapping and bird halitosis. De Musset envies the past, doesn't he?'

'Fantasy?' Ralph said. He had the feeling that Mavis was talking around the real topic she wanted to discuss, a devious, seemingly rambling, verbose introduction. Tasteful kept trying to drag her back to the topic that fascinated him, the double murder, but she ignored him.

'And then there's the pic of Piaf over there,' Mavis said. 'Her belter of a song: "*Non, je ne regrette rien*". That's the past completely gone but cherished all the same with a double negative. The French are like that, aren't they – super-generous with their negations? Piaf regrets nothing. I don't know what she'd done – maybe farted in a crowded lift – but so what, it turned into a bestselling single.'

'A brave and happy view of the past,' Tasteful said, 'but it isn't always going to be like that. The garrotting, et cetera, come into it, don't they?' We can't reasonably sit here, sipping away at magnificent stuff and pretend that garrotting doesn't exist.'

'How do you feel about this, Ralph?' Mavis replied.

'The past?' Ralph said. Did she mean the past with the two murders in?

'Would you have liked to be here in classical times?' Mavis replied.

Ralph wasn't sure. He'd certainly been alive at the time of the two murders, though, and the one of the undercover cop before them. He poured more of the sippable magnificent drinks. 'Of course, someone wrote, "The past is a foreign country: they do things differently there",' Mavis said.

'It isn't, though, is it?' Tasteful said. 'Pathetic inaccuracy. It's the same country but a little while ago and what happened then is still a part of now. We have to consider the garrotting and the other death on this basis, I feel.'

'It's a matter of mood,' Mavis said.

'What is?' Ralph said.

'The mood prevailing at the time,' Mavis replied. 'It might be able to justify something that happened then. But this mood may change and disappear. In these altered conditions, what could be regarded as OK not very long ago is not regarded like that any more. Oh, Timmy, dear, yes the past *is* a foreign country. For instance, people didn't seem to worry much about underage groupie girls hanging around rock bands. They seemed to think it was all very jolly to see underage girls fling their knickers at male performers on stage. We're more clued up now. The contrast gives us all those historic showbiz cases.'

'And then there's the current serene and impregnable Mr Iles,' Tasteful said. He had a smirk-type chuckle, the kind Ralph had noticed lately in others when they spoke of Iles. 'What was he up to in that foreign country – the past? People are asking, aren't they?' Tasteful said, 'TV producers included – forcefully asking.'

'Are they?' Ralph said.

'That's the word around,' Tasteful said.

'Around where?' Ralph said.

'Authority. Ministers. The Prosecution Service. As I understand it.'

'So, how *do* you understand it?' Ralph said.

'Perhaps it would be better to say how we *recall* it,' Mavis replied. 'And as we recall it, two absolute career villains were nonetheless acquitted of killing an undercover cop. I can remember the atmosphere – surprise and shock, disgust and resentment. Keats might have believed Truth was Beauty and Beauty Truth, but I've heard a different definition: "Truth is what a jury believes".'

'But then the two villains are themselves found dead,' Tasteful said, and not just found dead – one found dead by garrotting. Naturally a major case is opened.[1] This is a double

---

[1] See *Halo Parade*

murder, one by an especially horrifying method. But nobody is ever arrested or charged. Lots of activity yet no apparent progress. Is it possible that the deaths of the two crooks were a bit of tit-for-tat revenge and rough justice, not to be looked into over-vigorously? The case is apparently allowed to go out of sight and concern.

'Even villains have families and relatives. Possibly one or more of them have seen the recent awakening interest in old crimes, old alleged offences. For them, and for the court, the two hoods are not hoods at all – or not for the cop killing, anyway – but glisteningly pure and worthy innocents who have been disgracefully treated by the blind-eyeing, not at all impartial law. So, has a widow, or a dad, or a great aunt breathed a complaining word to, say, a member of Parliament or Citizens' Advice or the press? Well, we've given it some coverage in *The Scene* already, but that's only local. I'm talking now about the investigative section in one of the national dailies or Sundays. They're always nosing around looking for some state of affairs that will justify a front-page headline starting with that one self-congratulating word: "Revealed!"'

Mavis said, 'One of those big-time London reporters, listening to the grievances, might ask, "Who was police Operations at the time of those murders?" The answer, short and blunt, is, "Same as today."'

Mavis repeated this very slowly. It mightily pissed off Ralph. She seemed to think he wouldn't see the significance. Ralph had come out from behind the bar to confer so generously and selflessly a spell of revo-type equality on people like Mavis, and now here she was acting not just equal but superior. God, ingratitude! God, presumption! 'Same as today,' she said again.

Then Mavis went into a pause, lips clamped, eyes briefly closed for concentration. These few seconds seemed to bring a change of direction. Eyes open, she said, 'Is my boy Tim right after all? Although the past *is* a different country, there can be powerful links with now. Do we see the drawing together of present and past in a single figure – that constantly on-the-scene officer – Assistant Chief (Ops) Des Iles?

'Obviously, a member of Parliament, or Citizens' Advice helper, or the media would find it almost unbelievable that an assistant chief constable could be guilty of these killings. But I fancy, Ralph, you'd say this is only a blind spot because they don't know Mr Iles.'

Yes, Ralph probably would have said this, or at least thought it, but he didn't want to be told what he'd say by Mavis Barry-Longville. Was it a sentimental mistake to have sat with them? Was she worthy of any connection to the magnificent 14 July?

'Perhaps Iles is going to get some trouble,' Tasteful said, the smirk nicely in place. 'They're coming to get him. I believe they're going to do a TV version of all this, names changed to protect the innocent. The pressure for a proper inquiry will become irresistible.'

Just then Walter Vores, late 70s at least and wearing a French flag like a kimono, climbed onto the bar counter carrying a microphone and opened up with the greasy Maurice Chevalier number, 'Thank Heaven for Little Girls'.

'See what I mean about the way time alters attitudes?' Mavis said.

Ralph had to circulate. He left the Cointreau bottle with Mavis and Tasteful but took the Kressmann's. By moving about among the membership he was accepting unusual risks tonight. It was to capture the liberated spirit of Bastille Day. But he must be alert. The Monty wasn't Ralph's only business. Some very focused people wanted him gone. They'd willingly pay to arrange it. What Mavis and Tasteful had said about a possible official move against Iles troubled Ralph. They didn't seem to understand what that might mean to the city and, more particularly, to Ralph. Although Iles was a piece of raw evil, he did keep the area from falling into chaos. If he was displaced, the current good, municipal tranquillity could disappear. Ralph might need to tighten up on security at The Monty.

Normally he sat at a particular spot behind the bar next to a kind of small desk in case he wanted to look over some paperwork. He'd had a thick, steel bulwark made to hang from the ceiling between the club's main door and his seat. It gave a degree of protection in case someone slipped in and tried a quick burst of gunfire to kill him. To make the steel buffer look a bit less stark he'd had it covered with enlarged, colourful illustrations from William Blake's *The Marriage of Heaven and Hell.* Some members found this showy and pompous, and occasionally one of them would open fire at it, usually when drunk, causing very real danger from ricochets. This was another on-the-spot expulsion matter. Ralph knew it would be ineffective to ban all handguns. He recognized that members must be able to threaten what was once called 'massive retaliation' if attacked inside or near the club. Deterrence, he believed in it totally. But if someone actually fired a gun in The Monty, and especially if they fired at the Blake and damaged it, as had certainly occurred, they could no longer be regarded by Ralph as fit members of the club, even of the club before its promised renewal.

He thought nothing like that was liable to happen that night, but those two, Mavis and Tasteful, had put him on edge. He decided he'd do two more very brief affability sessions with members in respectful honour of the Bastille overthrow and then get back behind his rampart. The price of liberty, fraternity and equality was eternal street-savvy.

FIVE

Next afternoon, Ralph drove over to see Mansel Shale. Yes, that stuff about Iles from Mavis and Tasteful had badly disturbed Ralph. It would also trouble Shale. As Ralph saw things, although Iles was unquestionably a loathsome bastard, he was a loathsome bastard who unquestionably kept the streets, pubs, caffs, massage parlours and disco dens of his domain more or less peaceful and more or less safe, except for occasional routine splinter-group turf battles, of course.

Ralph wondered sometimes if it was actually *because* Iles rated unquestionably as such a loathsome bastard that the streets, pubs, caffs, massage parlours and disco dens stayed reasonably peaceful and safe, and therefore good for business – including, Ralph's and Mansel's busy, nicely parallel companies. Most likely on account of being such a loathsome bastard, Iles scared many villains into deep, timid, furtive caution and they tried not to provoke him by causing trouble and danger to ordinary law-abiding folk in the city's streets, pubs, caffs, massage parlours and disco dens.

Ralph certainly hated Iles, but Ralph – and Mansel – also depended on Iles. Ralph recognized this as a juicy paradox, and did everything he could to keep it sweetly alive. That would entail keeping Iles alive if the situation ever required it, and definitely entailed keeping Iles in his gorgeously powerful and magnificently unregulated job. The Operations in brackets behind his rank description – assistant chief constable (Operations) – could be a fucking monstrous pest, but they also helped preserve Ralph's and Mansel's incomes at a very useful and improving level, despite persistent national economic deficit and general financial troubles. For their firms to boom and continue booming Ralph and Mansel needed civic calm and no fussy interference by the police. Iles saw to both.

Ralph and his family could not live on Monty returns only. He paid big fees for his two daughters at private school, even though, to his disappointment, no Latin or Greek was taught there. Then there were the costs of their ponies, stabling and riding, plus heavy repair and re-design work at Low Pastures, and some basic smartening up at the club, a small start on his all-out redemption project.

He wondered now and then whether he should change the name of The Monty once the transformation was complete to The New Monty. Would that be brash, though? Brashness Ralph detested. Also, the point about those top-rate clubs in London that he yearned to imitate – such as The Athenaeum or The Carlton – was that they had a long, impressive history. In fact, this helped get them their terrific reputation. They were not jumped up. If The Athenaeum re-launched itself as The New Athenaeum it would sound gimmicky and vulgar. And if Ralph rechristened The Monty as The New Monty it might suggest there had been something wrong with the venue when it was simply The Monty. There had, in fact, been something wrong with The Monty – some *things* wrong with The Monty – or Ralph wouldn't have felt the need for a change. But he thought it would be harsh to behave as though the present Monty and its membership were somehow lacking and inferior, although they obviously were.

'I've had some intimations, Manse,' Ember said. 'I wouldn't put it more definitely than that, but, yes, intimations. TV might be involved.'

'Intimations *re*. what, Ralph?'

'Iles.'

'He's the sort sure to set them off.'

'What?'

'Intimations. If someone in a crowd said to me, "I can feel intimations nearby, though I can't tell exactly what they're to do with", I would guess at once these intimations concerned Iles.'

'This is not a matter of the immediate present,' Ralph replied.

'I can believe there'd be intimations about Iles whenever.'

'And yet in some ways it *is* about the immediate present,' Ralph replied.

'Exactly my sense of things, Ralph.'

'What is?'

'Time.'

'In which particular?' Ember said.

'Iles will be evil and dangerous regardless.'

'Regardless of what, Manse?'

'Time. Any time.'

'This is a matter of the past suddenly coming back into play,' Ember said, 'so it does concern the present as well as the past. There could be a link.'

'There's a lot of that going on.'

'What?'

'Links.'

'There is,' Ralph said. 'It's dangerous.'

'If it's to do with Iles it's always going to be dangerous,' Shale said.

'You remember the garrotting?' Ralph replied.

'A garrotting is not something easy to forget.'

'This is the then-and-now problem, Manse. Finding the link, if there is one.'

'Who?'

'Who what?'

'Who's searching for the link?' Shale said.

'There are people who think they have a sort of holy duty to dig into bygones, or *seeming* bygones. Authorities. Police. The government. They wouldn't care about the difficulties they might cause us, Manse. You and I are not top of their worry list.'

'Indifference is what we get.'

'Worse.'

'Worse than absolute indifference?'

'Cruel,' Ember said. 'There's a poem that deals with this. I had to study it. I expect you heard I was doing a university degree course.' Ralph had decided that Tasteful's mother wasn't the only one who could cough up poems.

'You've always been quite a scholar, Ralph. Famed for it.'

'Ideas, Manse.'

'Which?'

'They're what universities deal with. I make sure my mind

is open. It's as if I call out to ideas, "Come to me! You are welcome."'

'This is so like you, Ralph. Positive.'

'It's why I said cruel. A poem I had to study at uni mentioned April was the cruellest month because flowers started growing then out of dead ground. See any resemblances to the present state of things, Manse?'

'Them poets, they have their visions, don't they, Ralph, known as inspiration and they write them down? This inspiration comes to them whether they might be on a bus, or having high tea. They can't control it. They don't *want* to control it. That's what inspiration is. It's like a free gift suddenly arriving and not at all expected. Poets are well known for inspiration, plus rhymes.'

'We usually think of April as a happy month, not a cruel one, but the poet says it's wrong to start messing with something that's over, such as the dead ground. Likewise, we most probably don't want nosy sods poking about in, for instance, the past of someone like Iles.'

'I don't think there *is* anyone like Iles, Ralph.'

'Approximate.'

'Does the poet know Iles?' Manse said.

'This is a poem called *The Waste Land*,' Ralph replied

'That would be just right for Iles. He'd really feel at home there. Did he do it?'

'What?'

'Make it a waste land.'

'We have to look after him, Manse.'

'Agreed. Looking after him we look after ourselves,' Shale said.

This was true, but Ralph wouldn't have put it so direct and plain. Manse could be like that, though. He owned a converted rectory and they were talking in his drawing room. The big grey-stone villa with its long, hedge-lined drive had become too expensive for the St James's Church to run, and Manse had told Ember he bought it at auction, cash down in elastic-banded bundles from a khaki canvas kitbag. Although Ralph saw some deep symbolism in this – religion routed by readies – he doubted whether Manse would understand. For Manse, a canvas kitbag was a canvas kitbag capable of getting stuffed by a noble quantity of fifties, twenties and tens.

They were sitting in leather easy chairs, with glasses of what Ralph recognized as high-quality sherry, the kind that wasn't asked for much by slurping members of the present Monty, but which would certainly be a favourite among the different class of clientele Ember wanted for the transformed, elevated Monty, or, possibly, New Monty.

Ralph thought Shale didn't really have the kind of face suitable for a former rectory, or, really, for any sort of dwelling with more than two bedrooms, but the rectory had seven. Looking at Manse's face, though, you could believe that he was exactly the sort who'd go to a property auction with enough cash in a kitbag to buy anything he liked that came up. *Oh, I think I'll stick this lot on a rectory today.* Ralph realized it wasn't Manse's fault he had his sort of shambolic face, and he would absolutely never say anything that might make Shale feel uncomfortable about his home. Ralph thought faces were a gamble, with a lot of losers.

'How do we look after him, Ralph?' Shale said.

'That's what I came to chat about.'

'Did he do it?'

'Nobody has ever been charged.'

'I know. But did he do it?' Shale replied.

'Never charged, Manse. That's what we have to keep in our minds, isn't it?'

'Is it? It's why they want to dig into it, isn't it, Ralph?'

Ember thought Manse could sometimes sound pretty stupid. He wasn't though. He wouldn't have had a kitbag full of enough cash to buy a rectory otherwise.

SIX

B etween them Ralph Ember and Shale controlled virtually all the city's recreational drugs business. To ensure equality they divided the districts between them, using a detailed, nicely sensitive system. This obviously allowed for varying population size, but also factored in the apparent wealth, or not, of particular localities, the number of clubs, pubs, cafés, higher-education centres, seminaries, conference halls; and the racial patterns and general age range. Some of these calculations were guesses, of course, but Ralph and Mansel tried to make them intelligent guesses based on careful observation and long-term knowledge. They frequently revised the arrangement to take account of new information. Flexibility – as Ralph said, they couldn't have believed in it more. This civilized understanding between him and Mansel made for a generally peaceful trade scene with both firms operating in their own similarly profitable areas and avoiding border trouble. Ralph especially was very alert to changes and potential changes that might put this excellent but fragile scheme in peril.

Anything that seemed likely to damage Assistant Chief Constable (Operations) Iles or remove him from his post here darkly threatened this happy, productive Ralph–Manse alliance. Ember knew Iles thought the drugs game should be legalized, and so did many others in positions of influence and power. To Ralph, it looked as though the assistant chief (Operations) had privately decided Ralph Ember and Mansel Shale could be allowed to get on with their businesses as long as they stayed clear of serious violence – 'serious' meaning murder, attempted murder, kidnapping, torture, eye-gouging, grievous bodily harm, wounding.

Ralph and Mansel did all they could to satisfy this condition, and especially concerning murder, attempted murder, kidnapping, eye-gouging, torture, grievous bodily harm, wounding.

'No blood on the pavement,' was their bonny, comforting shared logo. OK, there'd admittedly been some very bad episodes in Ralph's past, but now he detested what he called 'the vulgarity' of turf wars and their 'disgraceful animalism' and 'appalling waste'. Apparently, Glasgow had brazen, daylight killings by drug gangs openly in built-up areas. Well, Glasgow was Glasgow and a long way off, but when he read press reports of these murders it made him even more determined to maintain decent tranquillity and order here – a kind of bargain, unspoken but strong, with ACC Iles (Operations). Ralph might detest Iles as much as Ralph detested turf wars, but Iles offered smart compromise and helped crucially with Ralph's good livelihood. Ember recognized that he and his family might not have been so pleasantly settled in their manor house, Low Pastures, except for Iles (Operations), the strutting, unchummy sod.

Ember realized, though – and maybe Mansel also realized it – that if Iles were replaced, his successor would possibly – probably – do some rough new-brooming and ditch the Iles policy of limited, *quid pro quo* tolerance. In fact, Ralph feared that the replacement might be deliberately picked by the Home Office to piss on that Iles policy and reverse it, perhaps savagely reverse it. *The minister is minded to give Assistant Chief Constable (Operations) Iles a merry kick in the bollocks.* That might be the kind of briefing for the new boy or girl. Ministers often got 'minded'. TV grew alert when a minister got 'minded'. The government didn't favour legalization, and most likely would not feel lovingly towards Iles.

For both Ralph and Mansel the present masterminding by the ACC (Ops) produced about £600,000 each a year, and improving. Naturally, it was untaxed. How could it be taxed when the trade was still in theory illegal? To tax it would be to endorse it. Iles did quietly endorse it, but Iles was not the Home Office. He'd gladly confirm this. So would the Home Office, in fact, more gladly.

'Can we find these people?' Mansel said.

'Which?'

'Find them in time,' Shale replied.

'Which people?'

'Before they can do real damage. Once something like that gets started it can go anywhere, like wildfire.'

'Damage by which people?'

'The law crew trying to get Iles for the slaughters. Do we see them off, Ralph – put an end to their unnecessary, dirty plotting?'

'See them off in which sense, Manse?'

'In the eliminate sense. Remove them one to one or as a group. Either way, we provide the right quantity of rapid fire to finish them and finish the poking about. Kill. It would be a sort of . . . you know . . . what-they-call-it?'

'What they call what?'

'Like it was in the Balkans. Wiping out a whole lot.'

'Cleansing?' Ralph said. 'Ethnic cleansing.'

'Yes, cleansing, not ethnic but getting rid of the unwanted. Destroy them and others won't want to come in case they get the same. Yes, cleansing. Necessary. Purifying.'

There were times when Ralph did wonder briefly how the fuck he ever got associated with someone as periodically demented as Shale. 'I don't think it can be done quite like that, Manse,' Ember said, his voice gentle and instructive, as if explaining things to a half-stunned child. 'It has to be a lot more . . . well, roundabout, more schemed.'

'That's like you, Ralph,' Mansel replied.

'What?'

'Roundabout. It's plain you been to that uni down the road. They like what are known as topics, don't they, and then there's discussion in a roundabout way so as to keep it going until the bell says end of lesson. Lots of "but on the other hands" and "in that kind of ballpark". Myself, I never went to the university, though people might not realize that and, in any case, I'd rather do it with .9-mm Heckler and Koch shells these days. They sort of wrap everything up neat and tidy. I think Des Iles would like this idea. It don't leave any doubt.'

This was the thing about Mansel. He wanted to run his companies without violence, as Iles required, but if there was a threat from outside he would react in one way, and only one way: gunfire. His mind could get taken over. For this, there was a terrible explanation, and because of it Ralph always tried to be sympathetic, patient and tender – attempted to get him back to something near what was, for Mansel, normality.

Not long ago Shale's second wife and his schoolboy son, Laurent, were shot dead in a botched car ambush. Shale's teenage daughter, Matilda, had been in the Jaguar with them but survived, and she and Mansel lived alone in the St James's ex-rectory now. To Ralph this didn't seem healthy.

Mansel was real target of that attack, but the hired gunman obviously panicked, rushed the job, and made deadly errors. Ralph was sure the deaths had pushed Mansel's mind askew. He had retreated to religion, seeking strength and consolation. This didn't seem to have worked for long, if at all, though he'd told Ralph he didn't blame vicars because they had to keep their minds on litanies and that kind of 'sing-song, dignified malarkey in churches.' Now, he had returned to commerce, but with a frightening belief in the ever-ready power of small-arms fire. He had seen this power used against his family. It had been a mistake, but Ralph realized that didn't matter to Manse. He wanted some of it so he could defend his interests and himself. Plus, he seemed to be set on retaliation and a sort of revenge. It wasn't against the people who killed his wife and son. They were not around. But it was as if he had fashioned a general hatred for the kind of world and type of life that could wipe out his loved ones, wipe them out by accident. This made it worse – the disgusting randomness, as though his wife and son should be annihilated just for the sake of it, no real purpose. He seemed instinctively to think salvoes, rapid bursts, strafing, volleys, perhaps, in fact, some form of perverted reprisal. Mansel considered this was how to make things 'neat and tidy'.

Ralph knew that behind one of the very classy pictures hanging in this drawing room, Mansel had at least four hand-guns and ammunition in a wall safe. Interesting pattern of changes: the church couldn't afford the rectory and sold it to a considerable businessman at a knock-down auction: Mansel; then Mansel turned one of its main rooms into an armoury. Ralph thought there must be some sort of deepish lesson in that, some sort of wider truth, but he didn't feel it would be a pleasant or comfortable truth, so he left it alone.

Mansel fancied art, especially by what was known as the Pre-Raphaelites, in frames of genuine wood, not composite. The picture hiding his safe was a Pre-Raphaelite number, most probably. Mansel liked women's long tresses and there were plenty of those in Pre-Raphaelite paintings – often gingerish.

'OK, Iles is a bastard, but he got to have some credit on a fair's-fair basis. I ask, what was he supposed to do in them circs, Ralph?' Mansel said. 'What? Tell me what, Ralph.'

'Which?' Ember replied.

'Which what?'

'Circs.'

'The verdict. That insane mistake by the jury. As I remember it, Ralph, one of Iles's undercover boys gets killed by a couple of bumrag nobodies who had a smart QC. They're acquitted, so Iles decides he'd better see to this issue personal, a sort of duty, a sort of what we already spoke about – cleansing, purifying – and does both of them himself. Neat and tidy.

'I don't know if you get along to hear many sermons these days, Ralph, but I listened to a lot a few months back and there was one about a prophet in what's called the Old Testament where God wants to send someone on a job and the prophet says, "Here am I, send me." This was to tell us in the congregation to get out there and do God's work. But now it makes me think of Iles. He sees there is something to be done about a garrotter, such as garrotting him, but realizes he's the only one who can handle it, so he says to himself, "Here am I, send me" to get the rotten little shits – garrotter plus one – and because it's him talking to himself of course he obeys and goes and does it. However, there's an expansion element: Iles knocks off two of them, although the dead undercover lad was only one.'

'We don't know as fact any of this, Manse.'

'It's what they'll try to prove. They'll get Desy Iles in the dock and their line will be that he's a big-headed, arrogant lout who believes he's such a crucial figure that he is more or less the only one who can look after the reputation of the police. The worrying, tricky thing is that this is very, very near the truth. Iles would be terribly hard to defend, wouldn't he, Ralph?'

Ember wondered whether he'd been stupid to come for this chat on tactics. With Mansel these days you never knew what Hunnish ideas he'd fling at you. Moderation? You'd think if Moderation was a person and had a face he'd slice lumps out of it. Ralph found the change in him amazing, but real. It began with that shoot-up of his Jaguar and the two deaths there. He seemed ready at all times now to respond with out-and-out extremism, appalling, crazed extremism.

Ember said, 'Manse, it would be wrong for you to go armed, stalking people on the investigation.'

'I don't see it like that, Ralph. But you're on your roundabout, yes?'

'They'd be ready for you.'

'*I'm* ready for *them*,' Shale said.

Ralph saw that this crazy, shoot-first, blissful cockiness was the new Mansel, and the new Mansel might go bustling and careless into big danger, maybe leaving his daughter, Matilda, the sole resident of St James's former rectory.

'We owes it, Ralph.'

'Owe what?'

'Protection.'

'Who to?'

'Iles. He's made things comfy for us. We got to repay.'

'My thinking, Manse, was that if they found enough new evidence to arrest him and put Iles into court, we could send what's known as "testimonial letters" to the judge saying what a lovely, compassionate and public-spirited man and dad he is, despite the very untypical murders.'

'He's a total cunt,' Shale replied.

'Of course he is. But it's probably best not to highlight that for the judge.' Ralph thought that if he did write, he'd sign the letter 'Ralph W. Ember'. This had quite a load of dignity and clout, because it was the form of his name he used when writing to the local press about environmental concerns, especially polluted rivers, of course.

'Letters are OK and you know them pretty well, but maybe

something else would be needed earlier than that, Ralph, such as handguns. It's to do with honour, and honour is something we both value above everything else, I know. Where would we be without honour?'

'Well, yes,' Ember said.

SEVEN

'Well, yes,' wasn't really an answer, but Ralph wanted to close down that kind of bullshit topic before it got properly started. Honour? It had never come up before as a subject between Shale and him. Of course it hadn't. It was a wool word. They'd talked trade, the quality and supply of substances, street-level prices, bulk prices, mixers, profits, security, women, filthy competition from medically approved legal highs, import methods and tricks, their children's fat-fee schooling. There was no call for big-mouth, dangerous notions like honour. Ralph could OK the commandment, 'Honour thy father and thy mother', but he didn't think honour came into life much beyond that.

Mansel seemed to find Ralph's reply fine, though. He nodded three or four times as if to emphasize their strong shared esteem for honour. A mix of excitement and determination flooded that ramshackle face. He said: 'What we got to do, Ralph, is go and have a bit of a useful squint at it tonight.'

'At what, Manse?'

'Where it happened.'

'What?'

'The deaths – the shooting, the garrotting. They'd like to prove Iles did both, wouldn't they? That means they'll need to look at the location. Yes, it's been gone over and gone over and gone over before, of course, as a double murder site, but they'll have to examine it all from the beginning again. So, what does this tell us, Ralph?'

'Well, that . . .'

'It tells us exactly where to find them when they're doing it. They're going to be beautifully exposed. We can deal with them then and there, can't we, Ralph? We got that debt I mentioned to pay off, haven't we? Iles takes care of our interests, Ralph, and we got to take care of him as a special "Thank you, Desmond." Obviously, Ralph, this is not something we could say face to face. He would never admit he had anything to thank us for. So, we do it our own way. We can still hate the strutting, vile sod but he's necessary. And to keep him safe from these outsiders we get rid of them, don't we, Ralph? I can't see no other solution. Can you? No, because there isn't one. As a help with that plan, we got to know the layout of the death house in detail – windows, doors, walls, gates, hedges and, so important, somewhere we can lie waiting for them, somewhere with a perfect field of fire, Ralph, somewhere snug and spot-on.'

Oh, God, was this more of the new blowtorch Mansel? Oh, God, was this visit a disaster and shouldn't Ralph have known it would be and not come? He stayed silent for a good half-minute, trying to work out how to bring Mansel back to sense.

'Urgency,' Mansel said. 'Priority. What's that famous saying, Ralph? You're good at sayings, due to undoubted education.'

'Which saying?'

'In the military,' Manse replied.

'What in the military?'

'About . . . oh, you know . . . what-they-call-it.'

'No.'

'Recce . . .'

'You mean, "Time spent in reconnaissance is never wasted"?'

'That's it!' Mansel replied. 'Military, yes, but it's also got a point for you and me, Ralph, in the commercial area, which, of course, includes the Des Iles area.' He stood and crossed the room to one of the paintings – a red-haired girl in a long, off-white billowing dress – lifted it off its hook and placed it upright on the ground, leaning against the wall. 'Arthur Hughes,' he said. 'Always puts plenty of material in the frocks and robes so he can get a sort of swirling effect. Known for them swirlings, Ralph. Say Arthur Hughes to some fan of paintings and he or she will reply at once, "swirlings". Most of what are called Pre-Raphaelites liked garments with plenty of stuff in them. Plenty of stuffing, too. They were all at each other.'

Mansel opened a blue-doored combination safe that usually lay behind the Arthur Hughes and said, 'Heckler and Koch for you as well, Ralph? There are a couple already loaded here. High-grade weapons but choice of a gun is a very personal thing and I want you to feel free to pick. Maybe you'd rather the Walther. This will be only the recce we spoke about but we'd better go ready, I know you'll agree with that.'

'I don't think we're ready for gun choice and so on yet, Manse. There should probably be more detailed talk, more step-by-step planning.'

EIGHT

At home, Harpur stood up quickly, but not quickly enough, and was going to answer the front-door bell but Jill, his younger daughter, gave him a little 'Don't even think about it, Dad' wave and went ahead. She usually did get to the door first if she was in the house. She'd scamper towards it fast, her slight body bent in a crouch, as if to make things tough for snipers.

Quite a mixture of people used to turn up at Harpur's home in Arthur Street. He reckoned he should be easily available to anyone hit by crisis and kept his name and address in the directories. Some people disliked police stations and never willingly entered one. They'd rather go to an ordinary house in an ordinary, long street, like Harpur's. Iles regarded it as disgracefully slapdash to bring up daughters in such a poor setting and often mentioned this to Harpur among a spray of other slurs.

Almost invariably the callers came because something and/or someone in their lives scared them, perhaps badly scared them, perhaps had been badly scaring them for a long while: the trip to 126 Arthur Street showed ultimate despair. Jill would always want to find out what this deep, frightening trouble was. She knew how to ask questions and how to listen to answers, and she'd often invite the stranger in for a chat and tea.

Harpur might have preferred to deal with this first contact himself but there were times – like now – when he didn't get a chance. His older daughter, Hazel, described her sister as 'an eternally, shamelessly, repulsively nosy little cow.'

He, Denise and the two girls had been looking through holiday brochures of Italy in the big sitting room at Arthur Street. Some inexhaustible rap music on, though the sound was low. Jill had left the sitting room door open and he could hear some of the conversation between her and the visitor, a woman.

Harpur recognized the caller's voice, of course. It startled him. He must have missed the first of the doorstep words, though. Jill said: 'Yes, he's here. Excuse me, but you called him Colin, his correct first name. This being so, it sounds like you know my dad, owing to what could be described as the familiarity of the name.'

'Oh, yes, I know him.'

'For a long time? Or, perhaps, less?'

'A while. It's why I'm here now.'

'But I don't believe you have ever called here before,' Jill said. 'I would definitely remember someone so smart.'

'Thank you. No, indeed, never before.'

'Excuse me, but I don't know why you say "indeed". That seems to mean it was not possible for you to come here. Why should it be impossible previously? If you wanted to come, what could stop you as long as you knew the address? This question is bound to arise, isn't it?'

'You must be Jill.'

'Dad told you about us, did he?'

'And you have a sister.'

'Older. Hazel.'

'That's it.'

'Usually, when people come here, it's a personal matter. But it could also be what's known as a business matter.'

'I suppose it could be termed a business matter, yes.'

'What else could it be called?'

'Ah, here's your dad now.'

Harpur followed Jill out into the hall. He'd decided he must join them and offer an escape from the third degree.

'It seems an age since I saw you last, Colin,' she said.

He tried to work out the tone of this. Jill would be doing the same. It was slightly more than matter-of-fact and conversational, but only slightly. 'Yes, a while,' he replied, a fraction up from offhand.

'Forgive me. This is something of an imposition, I'm afraid,' she said.

'Not at all,' Harpur replied. 'We'd always be glad to see you.'

'We have a lot of callers,' Jill said. 'Dad likes that. He thinks

it keeps him in touch, which is important in his kind of work
– in-touchness is one of his specialities.'

'I wanted to talk about one or two matters,' the woman
replied.

'That's how it is for a lot of the people who come here,'
Jill said. 'If he's not in, Haze and I don't mind listening to
their stuff. It's important to calm them down and that kind of
thing. If they blurt things at us we don't mind because we're
used to it. Quite often, someone who comes here with a
problem has been sitting on it for a long time and when they
eventually decide to speak it will often come in a terrific rush,
like escaping from within.'

'Yes, I wondered if I could have a word with you, Colin,
about the situation.'

'Usually when people come here it's about a situation,'
Jill said. 'There are all sorts of situations, obviously, but by
now Dad has seen most of them, so he can often help.'

'And then, perhaps, I could watch the TV thing about it
that's due on this evening.'

'"The Forgotten Murders",' Jill said.

'Desmond has gone out, deliberately, I think, to avoid it.
I'd like some company. My mother's babysitting. I expect
you're going to watch it.'

'I asked if it was a business matter, Dad, but the answer
wasn't really very clear.'

'Borderlines can be vague,' Harpur replied.

'Which borderlines?' Jill said.

'Between various areas,' Harpur said.

'Which areas?' Jill said.

'Like whether it's business or not,' Harpur replied.

Jill said: 'In *The Godfather*, one of the Corleone mob is a
traitor and says "it was only business" when he's found out.
They shoot him just the same.'

'I hear a lot about *The Godfather* from Jill,' Harpur said,
turning to the guest. He was grateful for the small distraction,
so he could get his thoughts straight after a rough shock.
Obviously, it was true that Sarah had never come to 126 Arthur
Street before. It would have been inappropriate – or, something
stronger than that: to quote Jill, 'not possible'. Harpur's home

was absolutely off-limits for her. They'd had their meeting spots, but never here. Things between Sarah and him had finished way back, though, and she'd obviously decided discretion was not needed now. Perhaps she really had come about 'business'. Yes, borderlines were sometimes vague. Harpur could make a guess at what the 'business' would be. He said: 'We're being rather inhospitable. I think we should ask Sarah in, don't you, Jill?'

'Sarah?' Jill said.

'Mrs Iles,' Harpur said.

'Oh,' Jill said. 'You call Mrs Iles Sarah and she calls you Colin?'

'Best not be too formal,' Harpur replied.

'Is that all right?' Sarah Iles said.

'Well, yes, of course,' Jill said.

But Harpur could tell she felt mystified and uneasy. In a way that was only normal. Their mother had been killed[2] and Jill and Hazel tried now to make sure Harpur's love life followed what they considered to be the right sort of path, and *only* the right sort. His daughters considered Denise was entirely the right sort of path. They loved Denise and would hate to lose her. They worried constantly about her smoking. Also, they grew acutely anxious when women they didn't know about seemed to have a closeness to Harpur – 'Colin' – especially beautiful women, naturally. Sarah Iles was very beautiful.

Jill did the introductions. 'Denise, Hazel, this is Mrs Sarah Iles, the wife of Assistant Chief Constable (Operations) Desmond Iles. Mrs Iles, this is my sister that we spoke about, and this is Denise who lives here part of the year, but also sometimes in her room for students at the university building, Jonson Court, Jonson without an h because it's named after a poet and writer of plays, Ben Jonson, not Dr Johnson who did a dictionary and has an h.'

'And as well as all that I sometimes make the tea,' Denise said and went out to the kitchen.

---

[2] See *Roses, Roses*

Naturally, Harpur could see a complicated sexual tangle in Jill's little commentary. She might be conscious of some of it, but her voice stayed very matter-of-fact. There had, of course, been Sarah Iles and him, for a while. There was now Harpur and Denise. And Mrs Iles's husband, the ACC, used to undertake a strong chat-up campaign for Hazel, though she was only fifteen. Last winter, to look glamorous and racy, and to curtain off his Adam's apple, he would wear a crimson scarf loosely around his neck and shoulders if he came to 126 Arthur Street in civilian clothes. And he'd turned up at the house quite often, because of Hazel, though he'd pretend it was to do with work. But he seemed to have stopped targeting Hazel when he found she had a steady boyfriend nearer her own age. Even Iles might tumble into decency now and then. Harpur couldn't make out whether she was disappointed or relieved. *He* was relieved, though.

Jill said: 'I think you might be puzzled about Denise, Mrs Iles. I don't think she'll mind if I tell you about her while she's getting the tea. Most probably you'll be wondering is she just a student with lodgings here? The answer to this is, no. If it was only about having a room she would stay at Jonson Court. It's what's known as the long vacation, but the room would still be there for her if she said she wanted to do research in the library. What we would like – that's Hazel and me – what we would like is for her and Dad to marry, although she's only twenty and he is not so young. And I believe Dad wants that, too, not just sleeping together, which is part of it naturally, but much more than that. It's true, isn't it, Haze?'

Harpur could see her tactics. She wanted to tell Sarah Iles he was already part of the household and therefore absolutely unavailable, if Sarah Iles fancied a wander from her marriage.

'They can say for themselves what they want. They don't need you,' Hazel said.

'Who?' Jill said.

'Dad and Denise,' Hazel said.

'I thought it would help if I explained things for Mrs Iles,' Jill replied.

'No need,' Hazel said.

'To me it seems like an emergency because she's never

come here before,' Jill said. 'Therefore we have to give her the full picture.'

'Of what?' Hazel replied.

'Of how things are,' Jill said.

'Which things?' Hazel replied.

'Here,' Jill said.

'She's grown-up. She can see for herself.'

'Not everything.'

'Why not?'

'Oh, you know, Haze.'

'No.'

'Yes you do,' Jill said.

'No,' Hazel said.

'Oh, Hazel is embarrassed,' Sarah Iles said. 'I think I get it. Did Desmond foolishly try something on with you, Hazel? Such an egomaniac dolt.'

'He had a red scarf,' Jill said, 'sort of dashing and romantic.'

'Quiet, dung-beetle,' Hazel replied.

Denise came back with the tea on a tray. She and Hazel sat on the chesterfield settee, Harpur, Sarah Iles and Jill in red leather easy chairs.

Sarah said: 'It's to do with the rumours about a possible reinvestigation, Colin. I felt I had to talk to someone in the know.'

'Which rumours?' Jill said. 'Dad hasn't told us about any rumours.'

'Concerning Desmond,' Sarah Iles said.

'How concerning him?' Hazel replied.

'Haze is bound to be interested,' Jill said.

'Gob shut, please,' Hazel said.

'A double murder, one a garrotting,' Sarah said.

'I remember reading about it in the papers,' Denise said.

'I think it was on TV news,' Jill said.

'We never got anyone for it,' Harpur said. 'The file's still open.'

'What does that mean?' Hazel said.

'Unsolved,' Harpur replied.

'What's known as historic,' Jill said.

'Cases get re-examined,' Denise said. 'Are they going to do this one?'

'That's the rumour, isn't it, Colin? And I gather television is doing something about it tonight. This is not a news report, because it's no longer news. But it's going to be a drama based on the facts.'

'Rumour, yes. That's what it is,' Harpur said.

'But why should this trouble you and bring you here, Mrs Iles?' Hazel said. 'Is it because he was in charge at the time?'

'Well, of course, he *was* in charge at the time, but possibly more than that,' Sarah said.

'More in which way?' Hazel said. But to Harpur her voice sounded as though she knew in which way.

'Not *just* because he was in charge,' Sarah said. 'Is he involved in the aftermath double deaths?'

Harpur said: 'It's all rumour and only rumour. This sort of thing comes up all the time in policing.'

'Which sort of thing, Dad?' Jill said.

'What's rumour, what's facts,' Harpur said.

'What *are* the facts, then?' Jill said.

'The full facts about the murders are not known,' Harpur said, 'or, obviously, there would have been charges.'

'Why are the full facts not known?' Jill replied.

'It's how it can be sometimes,' Harpur said.

'Why?' Jill said.

'Murderers don't usually come along and confess,' Harpur said. 'We have to find them, and find the evidence. It can be difficult.'

'You haven't got the evidence for who did those two?' Jill said.

'Some murderers can be extremely clever,' Harpur replied. 'But, as I said, the file is still open.'

Hazel held up a hand as if to say 'Cut the blah and listen.'

'Dad, do you know what all this seems to say?' Hazel asked. 'It seems to say people in some government office, or some editor, or some TV chief think Des . . . think Mrs Iles's husband, might have done the two murders as revenge for the death of an undercover officer, and so demand a new investigation by outsiders.'

'Yes, I thought that, too,' Jill said.

'Thank you *so* much but I don't need your opinion,' Hazel said.

'*I* wonder along these lines, as well,' Sarah Iles said. 'It's why I've come to see you today, Colin; I'd like to ask whether you know or suspect there are people – the people behind these rumours – who are out to get Desmond, ruin him by suggesting a link to the double killings? Is there a sophisticated, malign, destructive scheme? And, if so, it's possible, isn't it, that they want to get and ruin *you* at the same time? They'll hint you deliberately failed to run a proper murder inquiry because you had no wish and no aim to find the murderer. When these people consider Desmond they see someone who, in your words, Colin, is "extremely clever", and who knows a bit about detection and how to thwart it. They might float the idea that, if two crooks kill an undercover cop, someone – Des, for instance – might decide out of perverted *esprit de corps* and police comradeship that the pair deserve a privately arranged death themselves, especially if the courts declare them innocent.'

NINE

'Col, I would understand,' Denise said. 'Absolutely.'

'Understand what?' Jill said.

'If he tried deliberately to cover up for Mr Iles,' Denise said, 'if there *was* something to cover up.'

'Such as the two deads?' Jill said.

'Don't talk TV Detroit gangster, please, Jill,' Harpur said.

'Yes, the two deads,' Denise said.

'Do you mean that would be OK – the killings, and then only a sloppy, useless go at solving the case?' Jill said.

'It could be,' Denise said.

'How could it be?' Hazel said. 'Oh, how?'

Harpur thought she sounded deeply eager to believe Denise, but couldn't. He felt pretty much the same. Could anyone believe it? He still wondered whether the investigation of the two deaths had been weak – unconsciously weak – because of the possible danger to Iles. Harpur found it strange to hear this discussion take place as if he wasn't there. True, his daughters often talked together as though he wasn't present, and he'd regard that as standard behaviour between children and parent. But Sarah and Denise were here now and the subject matter very possibly enormous.

'Revenge,' Denise said.

'Yes, of course there's probably a revenge element,' Sarah Iles said. 'Revenge can be respectable. "I will repay," saith the Lord." Although the Lord doesn't come into it here.'

'Not just an element. Crucial,' Denise replied. 'It explains the lot.'

Denise had learned how to be ruthless in arguments. She was used to uni seminar argy-bargy about fine points in French poems.

'Revenge might not be lawful,' Sarah Iles said. 'In fact, generally it isn't if it entails violence.'

'Oh, stuff lawful,' Denise said. She waved one hand, a cigarette two thirds smoked between her fingers. It wasn't a stuffing movement but a sweep-away, get-out-of-my-sight shove. Harpur loved it. The bombast made her sound so young and thoughtless, and the ciggie showed acute dependency – on smoke. Didn't it all mean there was room for him to help her move on?

'Lawful – or not – matters,' Sarah Iles said.

That kind of polite, mild, thoughtful style Harpur remembered as typical of Sarah. He found it strange to hear the two women who were, or had been, his lovers cross-talk like this, part of that complicated sexual tangle he'd noticed earlier. As tangles went, this was a happy one for Harpur. Tangle on, you tangles! To see Sarah and Denise both present brought a tonne of extra life to the room, a grand improvement on the time when Harpur's late wife, Megan, had all her fucking books on flagrant shelves in here. Harpur thought there was definitely a place in life for books, but this room wasn't it. A decent while after Megan's death, he'd got rid of most of the books to second-hand dealers and had the shelves removed.

'Maybe some forms of revenge are not lawful, but are morally OK, entirely virtuous, even necessary,' Denise said.

'Yes? Honestly, Denise?' Hazel said.

'You want to hear only good things about the gorgeous Desy Iles, don't you, Haze?' Jill said, her voice oozy, mock-sympathetic.

'Keep out of it, Most Reverend Yobess,' Hazel said.

'Muhammad Ali,' Denise replied.

'What about him?' Sarah Iles asked.

'Let's recall what he said,' Denise answered.

'Regarding what?' Hazel said.

'Revenge,' Denise said.

'So, what *did* he say?' Jill asked. 'He was so great.'

'He said, "I believe in the eye-for-an-eye business." He couldn't respect a man who didn't hit back,' Denise said.

'You think Desmond was hitting back?' Sarah Iles said.

'Perhaps he wanted to vindicate himself,' Denise said.

'Vindicate himself? Desmond?' She made it sound as though 'vindicate' meant 'declare himself Sovereign'. 'He'd never believe he needed that,' Sarah said. 'Des believes that whatever is *is* right, as long as he's the one doing it.'

'As I see it, he knowingly puts an undercover man on a very perilous job and the cop gets rumbled and executed,' Denise said. 'Possibly, the assistant chief thinks he's got to hit back or he'll lose respect in the ranks and elsewhere. And possibly he does hit back and does it double, to make sure the lesson is clear.'

'What lesson?' Hazel said.

'"Mess with me or mine and here's what you get",' Denise said.

'You have information on this?' Sarah said.

'I had to study the topic at uni,' Denise replied.

'Which topic?' Hazel asked.

'Revenge,' Denise said.

'There are sixteenth-century plays about it, aren't there?' Sarah Iles said.

'They show good people striking back against vile enemies,' Denise said. 'Hamlet. He thinks he's got to kill his uncle because his uncle killed his dad and screwed his mum. "The time is out of joint," he says, and regrets he was born to set it right. Notice those words – "to set it right". He's the opposite of what you said, Sarah.'

'Which?' Sarah replied.

'"Whatever *is*, is *right*." Hamlet thinks you've got to work at it.'

'Do you think the assistant chief is like Hamlet?' Jill asked. 'Hamlet's the one who meets up with a skull in the graveyard, isn't he? Des Iles would enjoy this: no talkback from the skull.'

There'd always been a bit of a literary flavour about this sitting room. When Megan was alive she'd had the full bookshelves on three of the walls and this used to depress Harpur: it seemed to turn a house into a library. Some of the books had difficult or murky titles – *U and I*, *Edwin Drood*, *The Rule and Exercises of Holy Dying*, *Old Fortunatus*, *The Virtues of Sid Hamet the Magician's Rod*. They were so weird they'd burned their way into Harpur's memory. After his wife's death, and following that quite considerate, respectful pause, he'd got rid of the shelves and the books, except for a couple Jill wanted: *The Sweet Science*, about boxing, and *The Joe Orton Diaries*. He was fond of the sitting room now.

Today it seemed bursting with cleverness and knowledge. He didn't want to interrupt.

It was great to hear Sarah's voice again. She would be in her mid- or late-thirties by now but her skin was unlined and her fair hair had kept its shine. It was cut at just above shoulder length with a fringe, the mode nicely framing her face. Her eyes were grey-blue and very alert, intent on the conversation. Harpur wondered what she made of Denise. Perhaps she'd heard of her from Iles and so wasn't wrong-footed by finding her installed here. Or, at least, Sarah didn't show any sign of shock. Harpur thought she'd probably found the lecture on revenge very clunky, but appeared to listen. Most likely she was familiar with this scholarly stuff, but didn't try to compete. She looked good in a lightweight navy skirt and ivory-coloured top. She shifted about in her chair to face whoever was talking or listening and occasionally, and very briefly, because of a particular angle of her body, Harpur thought she might be showing an early sign of pregnancy.

'A part of our brain stops most of us from behaving on irrational, wild impulse,' Denise said. 'That's why Hamlet hangs about for so long, thinking he should get on with it, but doesn't. That special sector is in the brain's front area. It orders sensible, inactive caution. In other revenge plays, though, characters can lack this influential helping of grey matter. We had a lecture on all this to explain dark and bloody Jacobean drama. The characters become what's known in psychology now as "disinhibited and compulsive." That is, they don't suppress violent, maybe illegal, urges. In fact, they *can't* suppress them. Of course, those revenge play writers had never heard the modern jargon phrase "disinhibited and compulsive", but they understood the condition by instinct, by genius. Characters in their plays just go ferociously at things regardless.'

'Regardless of what?' Sarah said.

'The law,' Denise said.

'Assistant Chief Constable (Operations) Iles *is* the law,' Jill said.

'But you think that bit of his brain is missing, the restraint, inhibited bit, although the rest of it is so brilliant?' Sarah said.

'It's how people in most of the revenge tragedies behave,' Denise said.

'And Mr Iles?' Hazel said. 'You think he had an honourable mission and performed it?' She smiled. It was a gloat. Harpur had to recognize she did have feelings for Iles. They lingered. They went beyond the crimson scarf.

'Good old Desy,' Jill said. 'It should be two-eyes-for-an-eye.'

'The revenge tragedy heroes don't mutter like Hamlet, "Now might I do it", but don't do it. They do it,' Denise said.

'But will they see it like that?' Sarah said.

'Which "they"?' Jill replied.

'The people coming to do the reinvestigation,' Sarah said. 'For them, murders are murders. They don't believe in righteous revenge, except for God: "'Vengeance is mine,' saith the Lord." That seems to mean *only* "mine". And then there's John Milton in one of his poems. He seems to give the revenge job to God. "Avenge, oh Lord, thy slaughtered saints."'

'But maybe the snoops won't come,' Hazel said. Her voice had lost its bounce, though. Harpur thought he heard a touch of panic. 'This is only rumour, isn't it, Dad? There's a lot of gossip about it, but it *is* gossip, *isn't* it?'

'All of it, rumour,' Harpur said.

'I worry,' Sarah said. 'Desmond worries.'

It pissed Harpur off to see how much she and Hazel fretted about Iles, especially in this room that Harpur prized so much now.

TEN

He was naked walking fast to a mirror hanging on the bedroom wall just before the bullet that killed him broke open his head from close behind. He'd unhooked the mirror, had it in his two hands. Of course it went down to the floor with him and smashed underneath his body. But it didn't splinter into smithereens with a wide spread of bits and a delicious multi-crack noise. It snapped neatly across the middle into two, only two, possibly because the glass was high grade in this splendid property and did its terrific but hopeless best to stay intact.

He was holding the mirror in front of him at head height, so he'd probably have seen there the raised arm, the revolver, perhaps even the finger curled around the trigger, but after that not much else. The bullet was soft-nosed, a dum-dum, penetration limited. It didn't exit but nestled in the wound, like duty done, and easily recoverable. An ordinary round might have hurried on and burst out through the brow or an eye socket. It would have hit the mirror just before it fell, then most likely ricocheted to almost anywhere in the room and be hard to find – probably dug into the wallpapered masonry. This was an impressive, large, spruce room, reassuringly tidy, at least until the bare-arsed body with a segment of head now missing dropped dead there accompanied by the mirror.

Did he have time to yell before collapsing – a plea, a name, maybe, a curse? As well as the gun-arm and the revolver did he get a looking-glass glimpse of the face they belonged to? Had he recognized it? Man's? Woman's? Did he understand in the half a second available why this man or woman wanted to kill him? Perhaps something was said that explained it. Had he expected the attack?

The mirror – why had he gone for the mirror? It wouldn't have been to ask, like in the fairy tale, 'Mirror, mirror on the wall, who in this land is fairest of all?'

But suppose he had been taught or trained to believe that wherever you might be if you felt in deep danger and seriously threatened you could look around and almost always find a make-do weapon, something you could use to protect yourself. If he'd had time to turn with the oblong mirror in his hands, perhaps he could have swung it like an axe or broadsword, its metal frame giving quite an effective nudge to someone's neck, or knocking the gun into harmlessness across the room.

He must have felt for a minute that nothing real or actual existed, only dummies in the glass. He'd see his own face and the one behind, both enclosed inside the tight bounds of the mirror, versions of two people, but not people – copies, figments. This picture show didn't last – as most picture shows don't. He couldn't have known that, though. His very real actual gut flesh was pressed against real and actual glass on the real and actual magnificent, almost certainly hotel-quality, light blue carpet now due for some colour-clash staining.

There was no movement by the man prone there. His arms still stretched out in front of him, as they'd been when he held the mirror. He didn't hold it any longer. His hands were empty. This had been an execution: quick, very capable, perfectly adapted to the situation and the chance it gave. There couldn't have been a rehearsal in detail because nobody would have known he'd make for the mirror, maybe not even himself. That had surely been last-resort desperation.

Surely. Yes, surely. Or, surely? It was a guess by Ralph Ember, but, he believed, a very reasonable guess. In the television room at his manor house, Low Pastures, he was watching 'The Forgotten Murders', what listings billed as a 'reconstruction of events that would eventually lead to three murders, beginning with the death of undercover police officer, Detective Constable Raymond Street. Tactfully, the camera had trailed the naked figure from behind when he was walking across the room. Bare arses were OK on the main channels, though only briefly and not a lot of them.

In some ways the programme was a documentary and carefully factual. But not all the facts were known and available for this 'reconstruction', and 'in some parts of the programme, fictional material has been introduced to help make the course of events easier to follow.'

This meant that now and then the broadcast was more like a dramatic play than a documentary. 'But these additions have been fashioned with a strict and responsible attention to likelihood,' according to a programme note. So, the mirror and the bullet and the almost certainly hotel-quality light blue carpet were fact and, of course, figured in the trial. But the motive for taking the mirror off the wall, and the boom-boom, woolly thoughts about actuality and non-actuality were not fact and Ralph had to do some imagining.

So did the TV programme-makers. Now and then a voice-over supplied commentary to what was happening on screen, but couldn't always help. 'It is possible that if Raymond Street was holding the mirror in front of him, having just lifted it from the wall, that he would have seen the face of his murderer in the glass. We cannot tell whether Street knew the assailant who must have been standing close behind him to inflict that head wound.'

The camera focused hard on the pistol, and the gun-arm, but showed nothing that might reveal what the owner of that gun-arm looked like, face and physique, nor of which sex. The arm was of middling width and could have been a man or woman's; likewise the trigger finger.

Two men had been accused of Street's death, but had been acquitted. This left the identity and gender of the killer or killers unknown. The TV writer and director had to be careful here. Accuracy was impossible because they didn't have the facts to be accurate with. All they could offer was enigma, blankness, discretion.

Ralph reckoned that some people watching would ask why – why after so long – only enigma, blankness, discretion, especially as they were going to get another helping of enigma, blankness and discretion when the TV 'reconstruction' reached another couple of related, unsolved murders.

Among those asking the questions might be powerful figures in, say, the Home Office and/or the Crown Prosecution Service, whose job was to see that law and order functioned as they ought to function. Rumours said, didn't they, that there was already big dissatisfaction in the authorities, even suspicion, about how these crimes had been dealt with? Most probably the television show would sharpen that dissatisfaction, give it extra drive. Perhaps – a grim, very chilling 'perhaps' – it would lead to the kind of renewed investigations and unpredictable results that Ralph feared as a grave business threat, and had called at the ex-rectory to discuss with Mansel Shale. The outcome of that meeting remained uncertain. Mansel had shown off the pistols but Ralph thought the situation might be a bit more complex than Mansel realized. Shale didn't go in much for complexity.

ELEVEN

'"The mirror crack'd from side to side",' Denise said.

'Yes,' Harpur replied. At 126 Arthur Street, he, Denise and his daughters were also watching 'The Forgotten Murders' on television. Denise would be going to the gym when the programme had finished and was in a navy blue jogging outfit. Harpur thought she looked very competitive. She could always win him.

'"The mirror crack'd from side to side,

'The curse is come upon me,' cried,

The Lady of Shalott",' Hazel said. 'It's a poem, Dad. Tennyson.'

'James Thurber, a sort of funny writer, joked it was to do with feminine hygiene,' Denise said.

'Is that really how it happened?' Jill said.

'The body was found with the broken mirror under it, yes,' Harpur said. Their conversation paused while the television camera lingered on the posed death scene. When it switched to décor shots suggesting a large bedroom, the talk picked up again.

'Was it, like, kinky,' Hazel said. 'Naked, a mirror – narcissistic?'

'What's that?' Jill said. 'It sounds horrible.'

'Fancying himself,' Hazel said. 'Narcissus in love with his reflection in a pool. Classical tale. We did some of them at school.'

'But he could have looked at himself in the mirror if it was still on the wall,' Jill said. 'That's what mirrors on walls are for: to be stared at by people and show them how they look.'

'Perhaps he wanted full-body length,' Hazel said. 'He could stand one end of the mirror on the ground and hold it in front of him.'

'But why?' Jill said.

'Perhaps that was his special thing,' Hazel replied. 'Everyone to their taste. Heard of "full frontal"?'

'We don't know why,' Harpur said.

'Maybe he needed some kind of weapon, *any* kind of weapon, and nothing but the mirror was available,' Denise said.

'Why would he need a weapon?' Jill said.

'Somebody in the room wanted to kill him,' Hazel replied.

'You mean he knew that?' Jill said.

The voiceover gave a sort of answer to this and they stopped talking again to listen: 'It's possible that if he was holding the mirror in front of him when he'd just lifted it from the wall, that he would have seen the face of his murderer in the glass. We cannot tell whether he knew the assailant, who must have been standing close behind him to inflict that head wound.'

'We thought we did know,' Harpur said. 'The jury wouldn't have it, though, and acquitted those two.'

'And then the two were killed themselves, weren't they?' Jill said.

'They were, they were,' Harpur replied.

'It looks sort of . . . well . . . sort of neat, doesn't it?' Jill said.

'Neat how?' Hazel said.

'Like tidying up,' Jill replied.

'Tidying what up?' Hazel said.

'Those two,' Jill said.

'Which two?' Hazel replied.

'The two who killed Mirror Man,' Jill said. 'One pulling the trigger, the other helping in some way, known as "an accessory".'

'You haven't been paying attention, have you?' Hazel said.

'To what?' Jill said.

'To what the court decided,' Hazel said.

'You mean that it found them not guilty?' Jill said.

'Of course I mean the court found them not guilty,' Hazel said.

'Oh, that!' Jill said.

'It could be important,' Hazel said.

'Yes, it could be, but is it?' Jill replied. 'That's why I said "tidying up".'

'You think that killing two innocent people tidies things up, do you, Jill?' Hazel asked.

'Oh, innocent?' Jill said.

'There was a proper trial and that was the verdict,' Hazel said.

'Oh, verdict,' Jill said. 'I know what you're afraid of, Haze.'

'Afraid?' Hazel replied.

'It's loyalty,' Jill said.

'Loyalty? Who to?' Hazel said.

'I think it's *really, really* nice of you, Haze.'

'What is *really, really* nice of me?' Hazel said.

'You don't want those two *innocent* ones to seem guilty,' Jill said.

'Why don't I want those two *innocent* ones to seem guilty?'

'Because then it would look like they were killed as vengeance,' Jill said.

'Why would it?' Hazel said.

'Vengeance would be needed, wouldn't it, because the court made such a rotten mistake? Otherwise, those two would get away with it. And they mustn't be allowed to get away with it.'

'"Mustn't"? Who says they mustn't?' Hazel replied.

'Ah! If it's vengeance, we have to ask who would want vengeance and would be clever and brave enough to get it? We all know the answer, don't we? But you would hate that answer, Haze.'

'Not "look like they were killed", Jill, but "look as *though* they were killed", and so on,' Harpur said. 'Grammar.'

'Haze worries about Desy,' Jill replied.

'Why does TV have to go into all this in a pretend programme, Dad?' Hazel said. 'Don't they know it might cause bad trouble?'

'They like causing bad trouble,' Jill said. 'They're failures if they don't cause bad trouble. It's what they call *relevance*, meaning about what's known as *issues*, real issues, now issues, today issues.'

TWELVE

At Low Pastures, Ralph's wife, Margaret, had come and sat with him in the TV room for a while but didn't seem gripped by 'The Forgotten Murders' and left after a quarter of an hour. Margaret was clever, very clever, but he wasn't sure she'd grasped why this screen version of events mattered so much to him, mattered as a dire fucking pest and peril.

But, whether she grasped this or not, Margaret stood, raised two hands in a surrender gesture, gave a little apologetic smile, and stepped to the door. Ralph considered there was something special about doors at Low Pastures. They had been part of the house from its very beginnings, centuries ago, most probably. At various times the Spanish consul and a lord lieutenant of the county had lived here and passed through these doorways. As anyone would expect, they were old-style solid timber, not some three-ply sandwich like today's flimsy sort. Ralph always felt that to go out of or enter a room, or out of or into the house, via one of these on its massive, cooperative hinges was a very definite statement, not just a move in or out or out or in. Absolute bloody boredom – was that Margaret's statement? Maybe. But foolish if so. Margaret was occasionally a disappointment to Ralph, though he would try not to show it and would certainly never speak of it. There were quite a few pluses about Margaret. He'd often remind himself of this. Ralph believed in being fair to her, and she probably deserved that.

In any case, though, he thought, she'd want to quit before telly did its screen version of the garrotting. That death had appalled her when she'd originally read of the two killings in the press. She'd know now that the episode was certain to come up in this staging. Didn't the programme's title more or less promise that? TV producers had scouted around for a sensational, public-interest topic and decided that 'The

Forgotten Murders' needed to be made *un*forgotten. A network showing would fix that, stir the publicity, perhaps interest some members of Parliament and investigative teams on national newspapers.

Yes, and Ralph feared this might lead to dangerous questions about where the assistant chief constable (Operations) featured in those historic events. After all, investigating a double murder ought to be a major operation And if, as a result of the renewed nosing and disclosures, things went disastrously for Iles, things might go disastrously for Ralph, and for Margaret and for the Low Pastures family home, and Ralph's juicy niche businesses.

He had explained some of this to Margaret but did she realize the full gravity? At any rate, she couldn't watch 'The Forgotten Murders' to the end, regardless of the blight this programme might bring to Ralph's and Mansel Shale's gloriously sturdy but multi-risk companies. She seemed unable to appreciate completely that Shale's and Ralph's fine firms existed mainly because Iles let them exist for the sake of peace on the streets, and, if he was removed from his job, this ducky helpfulness would also be removed: Iles couldn't see to that from jail. He'd be too busy guarding his back from those he'd put there earlier.

Ralph considered himself a long-term thinker. He planned. He tried to cope today with what the future might come up with for him next week. He regarded this skill as a precious, inborn flair, but also the result of experience in the rough-house world of advanced commerce. Margaret didn't have that experience. It would be wrongheaded to expect her to see things as sharply as he did. Ember would not totally blame her for skipping away like that and shutting one of those meaningful doors on him.

Ralph couldn't slip away. He felt compelled to seek out everything to do with the murders. He believed any revival of interest in them could bring big trouble. Vigilance, he must not let this fade. Duty, he must obey its insistent call. Duty was almost always a strong impulse in Ralph. What he'd describe as humble, but unconquerable, doggedness showed in his face and general manner. He knew that many spotted a remarkable physical resemblance between him and a youngish Charlton Heston when Heston was supreme: the *Ben Hur* and *El Cid* periods. Ralph didn't object to this comparison. He'd seen some of the star's films on one of the movie channels and admired the craggy boldness of Heston's features. It seemed to tell of determination, grit, confidence and integrity. These were qualities Ralph personally fancied, too; above all, integrity. He liked to whistle up a very notable display of them himself when doing substances deals with some of the mix-prone, two-timing, brazen, wholesaling sods he had to bulk-buy his trade commodities from. Integrity they'd probably heard of, but wouldn't ever let it get in the way.

Ralph had a glass of Kressmann Armagnac near and he took a good, uplifting sip now. This was the kind of distin-guished tot a Spanish consul or lord lieutenant might have downed while thinking about consular or lord lieutenant-type problems. Ralph enjoyed feeling he was in the company of those past eminent high-fliers.

He thought that, in fact, the programme did its garrotting scene very skilfully. Maybe the most important part was the choice of background music during the build-up to it, and the actual unrushed throttling. Although Ralph was fond of a pleasant tune, especially marches and tangos, he did not really know very much about music, but he'd make a guess that the piece selected was something playful by Mozart, or one of those other flibbertigibbety composers of his era. A woodwind instrument such as flute or clarinet or oboe domin-ated, with mellow little spurts that made it sound as though life was OK, even jolly.

Ralph regarded this as very powerful, inventive irony because of the undeniable enormous difference in tones. The music was light and cheerful, seemingly *not* at all a parallel with the garrotting. Probably no composer of any period would turn out a work specifically designed to accompany garrottings. It wouldn't be a plus to have his or her 'Choke Anthem' listed among her or his works. The script could have asked the actor playing the victim to drown the music with a shout or scream. Ralph realized that would have been crude and obvious, though. Instead, TV wanted the audience to sense that the man getting strangled would most likely decide life was not, in fact, OK and/or jolly, but fucking last-gasp painful as the ligature dug in, and the oxygen went missing, *his* life unlikely to go on much longer.

Ralph thought that at the TV headquarters they'd have true experts in music and when garrotting was mentioned as a tasty dramatic factor in 'The Forgotten Murders', one of them would perhaps say at once, 'I know just the sonata or rondo to tinkle a contrasting, cheeky partner to the dedicated neck squeeze.'

Of course, the cameras had to be very tactful and discreet again – even more so now. This was a public television channel. It must not horrify viewers by mocking up too exactly the supposed circumstances of the killings. There were no face shots in the death scenes, particularly not of the garrotted man's.

A deliberately very blurred, markedly out-of-focus figure carried out the garrotting and other killing. Obviously, this was what Ralph considered to be the Iles character, though he hoped he had that wrong. And if it wasn't wrong, he hoped it wouldn't be proved beyond any reasonable doubt right. There was quite a difference between what people regarded as true and what a court decided was true. Occasionally, Ralph wondered whether Iles might plead guilty, just for the kind of stuff-you laugh he loved, the malevolent bastard.

Ralph thought the television writer and director and those above them *wanted* people to assume this mysterious, almost spectral male was Iles, though that could never be told straight, either in pictures or voiceover. There was a law of libel, and an assistant chief constable (Operations) would know how to use it. Television executives aimed to bring to the present-day details of those forgotten murders, but without landing themselves in a present-day trial for staining someone's present-day reputation. No, not just someone's – an assistant chief constable's (Operations); and possibly an assistant chief constable (Operations) of sufficient clout, fight, and ample natural venom to perform a revenge attack with two murders, one a garrotting, though this could not be said or shown in case the assistant chief constable (Operations) sued for plenty. Ralph, in fact, believed Iles would never sue, whatever was said and shown.

He would regard any behaviour of that sort as disgustingly bourgeois and prim. But that was not a view TV executives would be able to take.

They'd picked an actor of about Iles's age and slight build, but that was as near as they went. The garrotting seemed carried out with imperturbable style and easy flow, and Ralph would agree that if Iles did it, this was how he would do it. Iles had developed persecution into a junior art.

The pattern of the death scene was not easy to imagine, but 'The Forgotten Murders' had to attempt a tidy re-enactment. It seemed to assume that the two men had been surprised by the murderer, who was armed and kept them covered. One man was forced to tie the other into a chair and was then shot, and the man in the chair garrotted. Ralph had heard at the time that a piece of coal had been jammed into the mouth of one of the men, but this was not shown in the television adaptation. No faces appeared, with or without coal, in the concluding part of the television adaptation.

THIRTEEN

In the big sitting room of Harpur's house, Sarah Iles bent forward from her chair, as if to get closer to the television screen and a better view, perhaps trying for a glimpse of some characters' fronts and faces, not the back of their heads. She was looking, of course, for her husband's stand-in; sure he would be here in this bit of theatre and praying that he hadn't been in reality.

At the moment the screen showed a man apparently tied to a kitchen chair by his ankles and with his wrists bound together behind him. Another man stood near but then moved swiftly around to the rear. He was carrying an automatic pistol, and in the other hand a metre-long piece of thin rope or electricity cable and what looked like a broken-off segment of broom handle. The camera pulled away then stayed for half a minute on a third man. He wore a suit and lay face down and unmoving on the floor.

'Oh God,' Sarah said.

'It's only make-believe, Mrs Iles, like a play or movie, isn't it, Dad?' Hazel said. 'Isn't it?'

'Absolutely,' Harpur said.

'Called faction,' Denise said. 'Very modish. A mixture of fact and fiction. Nobody really knows what went on, except the one or more than one who did it.'

'He must have gone there with lengths of something to get him tied with and killed with,' Sarah Iles said. 'And that pole or stick – to get under the rope knotted around his neck and twist and twist. Blatant, awful intent. It was all schemed, like an . . . well, like an operation.' These final words she spoke in not much more than a whisper. Harpur thought it was as though what she'd watched had wrecked her mind.

There was an advertising break during the programme and Harpur cut the sound by remote. Denise, who'd been sitting on the chesterfield with Hazel, stood and crossed the room to where Sarah Iles had a red leather easy chair. Denise knelt alongside it and took Sarah's hand. 'You're still thinking of it as real, aren't you?' she said. 'It's not. You mustn't get into a state. It's something cooked up to excite and convince and hang on to an audience. It's telly.'

'But it's accurate, isn't it?' Sarah said. 'That's how it was. The press said so at the time – a man tied to a chair and strangled, another man dead nearby.' Harpur found her voice still weak, but she got the words out somehow.

Denise let go of Sarah's hand, straightened and brought a packet of cigarettes and a lighter from her jeans pocket. She lit up and took a hard drag. Harpur knew this type of preliminary usually meant a few weighty words were on the way. 'Yes, that stuff is accurate, the sort of framework,' she said. 'Basics only. But what's upsetting you, Sarah – is it OK to call you that? – is the built-in suggestion that the man bringing the deaths is your husband, Desmond. It can't say so, but the suggestion's there, semaphoring itself to us like mad. And that's all it is – a suggestion. And suggestions can't be accurate because they're not fact. Some writers do two ends to a story – to see which works best. It's all variable.'

'Denise studies all this sort of thing in university, Mrs Iles,' Jill said, 'such as what really is reality. That might seem an easy one to answer because reality has to have what is real to make it reality and what is real is usually there to be seen. But she told me that what's known as theories exist about this kind of big thinking. Denise has to read the books of French tiptop scholars and follow their sharp way of seeing important matters and summing them up.

'Often when Dad is sounding off with some of his ideas, if he's been at *Reader's Digest*, Denise will mutter a couple of words – sometimes in French, sometimes English – and it will prove everything Dad's been saying for the last few hours is shaky. Dad doesn't mind this because he loves her. Honestly, I've never seen him get ratty and/or spit when Denise made him seem half daft. It's not just owing to great boobs. Deeper than that. He would never change Denise just because she knows awkward stuff from some of these Paris chew-the-cud gang over there, having a glass of red at a pavement café and discussing almighty topics with friends, such as the meaning of life, if it has one, and that kind of puzzler, while smoking Gitanes, just like Denise when she can get them.

'Some of what they talk about and write about in their books can be useful. Mrs Iles, they don't know you, of course, but their urgent, non-stop search for truth is about people everywhere. They help Denise see everything to do with this situation, so we're very lucky, aren't we?'

'Really?' Hazel said.

Denise went back to sit on the chesterfield.

Sarah Iles said: 'Have they been able to persuade the television people, maybe bribe the television people, to put on that programme, Colin, knowing it will cause damage?'

'Have who?' Harpur said.

'The crew wanting to destroy Desmond,' she said.

'Which crew?' Harpur said.

'He has enemies,' she replied.

'I should think all police have enemies,' Denise said. 'That's part of the job. The higher the rank, the more enemies.'

The screen advertisements finished and the final part of the programme began. Harpur restored sound. The camera focused on the outside of the police headquarters building. The assistant chief appeared at the main entrance. He was in civilian clothes. An unmarked car drew up and he climbed into the back and was driven away.

'Where was he going, Dad?' Hazel said.

'No idea. I wasn't there when they filmed him.'

'It's symbolic,' Denise said. 'They want to hint he's off to somewhere, anywhere, to get away from this case.'

'Haze still frets about Desy,' Jill said. 'She doesn't like to think of him out there in the world's big emptiness, alone except for a police driver.'

'Shut it, tadpole,' Hazel replied.

Voiceover said: 'Police still hope for progress in their hunt for possibly two killers. The investigation remains ongoing and new information is regularly added. However, relatives of the victims do not find it easy to accept these assurances. They would like the file closed, but not because the investigation has been abandoned, as they fear it might be. No, they long to hear the offenders have been caught, convicted, and locked up.'

'I liked her,' Denise said.

'Good,' Harpur replied. They were in bed. The house was dark. Sarah Iles had left and the children were in bed, too. Harpur had told Denise long ago about the affair with Sarah.

'But it seems strange,' Denise said.

'What does?' Harpur said. He thought he knew what, but it would be better if she said it.

'She comes to ask a one-time lover to help safeguard her husband. Weird?' Denise said.

'Who else could she ask?'

'And she finds her one-time lover with another lover,' she replied.

'You were kind to her,' Harpur replied.

'She looked distraught.'

'Scared.'

'Do you think Hazel and Jill realize?'

'Realize what?' Harpur said.

'That there'd been something between you and her. You told me, but I don't believe you'd have told them. They're smart, though. Is that why Jill made the speech?'

'Speech?'

'About you wanting only me and it's for more than my boobs. Also, you never spit even if I contradict you, because you love me.'

'I do want only you.'

'Good.'

'I want only you at this moment, as a matter of fact,' Harpur replied.

'And as a matter fact I want only you at this moment,' Denise said. 'Do you think that would please Jill?'

'I think she and Hazel take it for granted.'

'Good.'

'I would never take you for granted, though,' Harpur replied.

'Good. Just take me,' Denise said. She stubbed out half a cigarette plus in the bedside ashtray.

FOURTEEN

The heart-breaking damage at the club he owned, The Monty in Shield Terrace, plus the bad injuries to some of the members and bar staff, brought a terrible confusion to Ralph Ember. He had always been vulnerable to brain-cringe in a crisis, which was why some called him Panicking Ralph, or, worse, Panicking Ralphy – neither of them to his face. Although he'd thought he had grown out of that weakness long ago, here it was again and at first he couldn't see a way to fight it.

Dilemma. Oh, God, Ralph resented the mercilessness of facts, the jumble of demands on him: the club, the substances business, the family, the TV, the murders above all. If Iles was accused and put on trial, Ralph would feel bound to use his special influence to help him in all possible ways, and especially by very carefully worded, skilfully argued, sort of sincere, properly signed, letters to the prosecution, protesting the ACC's innocence and all-round stalwartness. It was crucial to save Iles and his policies because he kept the city peaceful and safe, perfect conditions for happy trading in a full range of the commodities. Ralph did realize that this might sound selfish – as if all that mattered was his personal happiness. But, no, it wasn't really like that. Ralph reckoned that if *he* had a contented, rewarding life, the whole city must be in a fine condition, too – peaceful and safe.

Suddenly, though, the city was not at all peaceful and safe: The Monty had been appallingly desecrated. Some even said the violence had been so large-scale it caused structural shifting. This was just the kind of deeply uncivilized incident he'd desperately struggled for months to avoid at The Monty. His well-known, grail-like plan to get the club up to the social and intellectual level of The Athenaeum, The Reform, or The Garrick in London would take a significant knock when news spread of that sickening, destructive shindig.

If someone in conversation mentioned his club, the response might be, 'Oh, yes, The Monty, that's the one where the woman's rib-cage was smashed by an upended pool table one party evening, isn't it? I think I'm right in saying it happened on the watch of ACC (Operations) Desmond Iles, aren't I? She needed operations, but not his sort.'

Ralph could understand why panic had returned and hit him so ferociously. He detested Iles, but had been prepared to support him because he was good for tranquillity and sales. Was he though, now? Why should Ralph try to look after Iles if the ACC couldn't see to his side of the arrangement? That was a neat bit of workaday logic, but it depressed Ralph. The city could not function properly without a dominant Iles.

But had Iles lost the knack or the will, or both, to dominate? Did Ralph have to look after himself and his club solo, unprotected? The idea unnerved him. Had his life and career been pleasantly safeguarded and smooth for so long that he had forgotten how to deal with major abrupt changes?

When he looked back on the grim events of that evening, Ralph realized that it had been an error to watch 'The Forgotten Murders' at home. Because of his absolute concentration on a single, stark aspect of things – the danger to Iles and therefore to vital and traditionally sheltered local commerce – he'd failed to see that 'The Forgotten Murders' programme might have a much wider effect than the demolition of ACC Iles. Ralph should have gone to the club for the viewing. He might have been able then to keep this evening's tension from growing more and more threatening. Even if he'd stayed at Low Pastures for the broadcast, he should have driven to the club as soon as it ended. He had delayed, though, kept back by a wish to think over what he'd watched on the screen about the murders but also by a kind of smugness, stupidity and lust.

He knew he ought to have recognized much more vividly than he did that 'The Forgotten Murders' docu-drama was liable to inflame all sorts of venerable jealousies, hates, and enmities. Although the murders might be forgotten, these adjacent loathings were not. Yes, yes, Ralph knew strong dislikes probably existed among members of the Athenaeum and

similar clubs, but they didn't petrol-dowse one another's jackets
or hair and set them alight. Ralph believed there had to be
acceptable standards. He regarded a club as like society in
miniature, and any departure from order was liable to tumble
into havoc. At The Monty that's what the programme aftermath
tumbled into – havoc. And at the centre of that havoc was the
unmanageable, insistent question of Assistant Chief Constable
(Operations) Desmond Iles.

Suppose this telly extravaganza did what it was obviously
meant to do, provoke a new inquiry leading to murder charges
against Iles. If Ralph's calculated help for him was to be effective, Ember's business and social status had to be generally
recognized – recognized and respected. It would be difficult
for this to work at optimum, though, if he became known as
proprietor of a mucky drinking club that could slide into
bloodstained, disgraceful anarchy without apparent cause or
warning. How would a prosecution team be affected by a letter
or letters from such a comically low-grade, guttersnipe source?
Answer: hardly at all. He could imagine them in their farcical
fucking wigs reading one of his letters and trying to guess
what the W in his signature stood for. 'Wanker?' one of them
might suggest, and they'd convulse from giggling. Saving Iles
and consequently saving the current, splendid, cherished
trading *milieu*, might be no longer possible.

Just before 'The Forgotten Murders' reached the final
credits, and also before Ralph had known of any problems at
the club, Margaret came back to watch the end of the show
with him. She held his hand. This really pleased Ralph. It
had hurt him when she left just after the programme began.
That silly 'I surrender' gesture she'd made irritated him. After
all, this programme could have a very rough impact on many
lives, including the assistant chief's and therefore hers, and
Ralph's and the children's.

But, besides this, there came a more personal matter. He
was someone with looks often compared by quite sensible,
unflattering folk to those of a one-time top-billing Hollywood
star. Ralph wasn't used to being discarded by women. The
reverse. They clustered around him. If there was going to be
an earthquake, as in one of Chuck Heston's films, Ralph was

the type they'd want to be saved by from under wreckage – his vigorous, talented hands everywhere, ungloved.

He had a scar down one side of his face. This did not spoil the resemblance to Heston, though. In fact it seemed to fascinate many women, and they would finger the mark quite energetically, as though it could be prised open and give access to Ralph's considerable inner being, so many fine, resolute impulses stored there on call. He wouldn't consciously seek this kind of quaint attention, bordering sometimes, he thought, on idolatry, but if it happened he didn't greatly mind. He felt he could not be blamed for the God-gift of his classic features, any more than a cheetah could be blamed for elegant, deadly speed in the hunt. Ralph's view was that a face had only a limited spell at its best, and this should be given maximum use. Perhaps jealousy explained Iles's childish malice. He couldn't do much about that mountainous Adam's apple. No wonder he liked scarves.

Margaret's return and the hand-clasp had told Ralph a lot. She'd obviously begun to appreciate that her behaviour earlier had been cruel, flippant and insulting, absurdly the wrong attitude towards someone whose resemblance to the young Charlton Heston could be checked on a movie channel and never reasonably disputed. She probably knew she shouldn't have made that *kamarade* signal. It suggested that he had her as part of a captive audience and wanted to force-feed her some TV tedium, whereas Ralph believed she longed to run gloriously free, like a fawn or Pekinese let off the lead.

Perhaps eventually she had worked out that Ralph would not be so tied to the telly unless what was being played out there had a crucial, possibly grave, meaning. She would know Ralph detested Iles. If she realized the programme was about him, though not named, she must sense something serious compelled Ralph to shelve personal aversion and learn what there was to learn about him.

Now and then, and particularly now, Ralph liked to make love to Margaret in the TV room, with the door locked in case the children tried to come in. Unlikely: they each had a bedroom telly over in the east wing of Low Pastures. It was crucial to Ralph that the television should be on while he and

Margaret were enjoying each other. He saw this as a way of declaring their independence. It didn't have to be a specific programme, just a programme. Ralph wanted to show their disregard for the clever people whose job was to make one programme glide easily into the next so watchers didn't change channels or switch off. Ralph preferred having it off to switching it off. He had an identity to take care of – his. He'd make his own choices, thank you. He knew there had been shaky aspects of his character in the past and he had to put that right – provide an update.

'The Forgotten Murders' had finished and there was something else on now. Ralph didn't bother to work out what it was – to do with health, probably; everyone had health, or didn't have it, so TV loved camera shots of scalpels and heartbeat charts and billowy green surgical gowns.

On top of this, Ralph longed to show how much he appreciated Margaret's decision to come back and sit so close to him, their fingers locked. He didn't want Margaret to feel excluded from any part of his life, especially a part she probably didn't totally understand – his obvious, compulsive concern for Iles. Ralph would prove even that could be put aside for her sake. He felt she deserved his generosity. He more than half regretted his rattiness when earlier she'd retreated from the room.

Ralph thought of himself as part of the large world outside, but she could be invited into it now and then. During his Foundation Year at the university he'd come across a poem by Thomas Hardy where he and his lover walked up a hill together. The hill had been there, of course, for millions of years. It was primeval. But the poet said the most brilliant event in this hill's story was that those two hiked on it. Ralph thought this was very like Margaret and himself. There was a wide background to their lives, but they were special, unshakable, secure in it.

Their lovemaking was joyful and silent. Neither mentioned Iles at any point. They were naked on an old but handsome uncut moquette settee, which had been left behind by the previous owner when Ralph bought Low Pastures. He regarded this settee as similar to the hill in Hardy's poem. Fucks were

better than furniture. Ralph thought he and Margaret gave the
settee bare-arsed distinction now, but he didn't rule out
the possibility that others, possibly even a lord lieutenant of the
county, had also brought a kind of impromptu passion to
the moquette previously. The impromptu quality was vital. It
wouldn't have worked to plan these lovely minutes. A kind
of shag itinerary. They had to be led up to by that bad instant
when she left, then the apologetic reappearance, the hand-
holding and the active, bright, stupendously irrelevant monitor
screen.

FIFTEEN

Ralph liked to go to The Monty a little after midnight and stay until it closed at around two a.m., unless there was a special celebration party for, say, a birthday or a divorce or Bastille knees-up, when it might stay open much later. First, he'd walk slowly with a torch around the outside of the building, checking for timer-set incendiary treats and/or bodies. He used the torch very carefully, more off than on and hand-shading the beam. If someone up late in one of the Shield Terrace houses or flats glanced out of the window and saw a light systematically casing The Monty, it might look very sinister, and he didn't want to cause more local anxiety than was unavoidable.

Although Ralph's manor house, Low Pastures, had spacious grounds on all sides, he did try to understand the problems that might bother more ordinary people huddled up in skimpy dwellings like those of Shield Terrace. After all, it probably wasn't their fault they lived in such places, and they lacked the skill and push to get out of them into something more worthwhile.

In fact, the light *was* sinister – not because Ralph patrolled but because he *had* to patrol in case some fucking business colleague or colleagues tried to flame-finish the club. Insurance brokers could not find any company that would take on The Monty coverage. This, naturally, depressed Ralph, but he knew it would be foolish to get in a full-out rage about it. The Athenaeum might never get refused insurance, but Ralph recognized that The Monty was not in this category, yet. Occasionally, too, the remains of someone killed in a gang spat were dumped in The Monty*'s* yard to bug Ralph in jokey style.

Also out of civic thoughtfulness for neighbours, when he had done his safety inspection Ralph would stand for a while in front of The Monty's main entrance, perhaps chatting to

one of the bouncers, but sometimes alone. He felt that any
watcher must surely be comforted to know the owner had
arrived: the captain's on the bridge. Most of the Shield Terrace
residents had probably seen him around the club in the day,
so they'd recognize him now.

He knew his resemblance to Chuck Heston made him very
memorable. In one of the Heston warrior films, *El Cid*, he had
played a great leader, and wonderful inspiration to his troops.
Ralph on the pavement outside The Monty at night thought
that here and elsewhere he had the same sort of role. He willingly accepted this duty, seeing it as a kind of charge set by
Nature for his beauty.

He always wore a custom-made double-breasted dark suit,
white shirt, blue fedora trilby, dark tie and button-hole carna-
tion for this late visit to the club. He thought his outfit suggested
orderliness and quiet decency. Some Monty members – Tasteful
Barry-Longville, for instance –went in for the same kind of
sober gear, and Ralph hoped to persuade others to smarten up
in similar fashion. Now and then, behaviour at the club didn't
quite reach the quality he'd like, but it was rarely outright
Hunnish. When he stood on the pavement like this for those
very meaningful few minutes, he had his back to the club
doors. He gazed away from The Monty and into Shield Terrace
and beyond. Partly this was to make his face reasonably
visible, identifiable by inhabitants. But, also, he thought it
would be a kind of vanity to spend this time looking at
The Monty frontage. Although Ralph was proud of the club, he
didn't want to carry on as if he could think of nothing else.
He was part of that world scene out there, the one he'd willingly
invite Margaret into with him because she undoubtedly
deserved it fairly often.

When he broke away from his contemplative spell and
entered the club, he took off the fedora and held it by his side.
This was a modest, unflamboyant movement, not a sweeping,
theatrical, extravagant gesture. He meant it simply as a polite
act of respect to the members, and there were definitely certain
members he did feel some respect for. Inside the club at his
small desk, beneath the *Marriage of Heaven and Hell* flying
slab, he'd do a quick look at the bar takings and bag some of

the cash for a trip to the bank overnight safe on his way home, varying the route.

Lecomte Biss, tall, cocky, sharp, was helping run the bar tonight. His first name, pinched from among titles in the French nobility, showed his parents must have imagined he'd land a great career. He was about sixty and hadn't landed it yet. He bent to talk directly to Ralph above the noise of the club. 'Ilesy,' he said.

'He's here?' Ralph replied.

'Was. On the telly.' Lecomte nodded towards the big wall monitor. It was switched off now. A quartet – horn, double base, clarinet and drums – had been playing for some dancers and would do their final stint shortly.

'Really? Local news? At some function? Was he in full dress uniform?' Ralph played ignorant. He had to show he needed evidence before he'd interpret the show. Barmen might be less strict. Not The Monty owner. Not Ralph W. Ember.

'A drama,' Lecomte replied.

'Which?'

'About two killings – unsolved. Unsolvable?'

'"The Forgotten Murders", you mean?'

'It was on the screen,' Lecomte said.

'I saw it at home. Interesting whodunit? How is the ACC concerned though?'

Lecomte gave a tiny, come-off-it-Ralph smile, but didn't answer at once. Then he said: 'It could be troublesome.'

'Troublesome how?' Ralph replied.

'There are people here tonight from both sides,' Lecomte said. 'I don't know whether it's deliberate or a fluke.'

'Both sides of what, Lecomte?'

'The deaths. Their friends, on one side. Maybe relatives. Guests of members.'

'Whose friends?'

'The deados. Their families are pushing for an inquiry, aren't they? And then – the other side – some people seem to think Iles did a fine, brilliantly helpful cleaning-up job. There was applause and big laughs when he saw off the two. I'd say those two deads probably ran a wholesale snort and needle firm and villains from a rival business are tickled to see them obliterated. It's a gorgeous free gift, chortle, chortle. More or less by accident, Iles – if it was Iles – did them a favour: removed two of the opposition. A couple of blokes performed twist movements in the air with their hands, like the garrotting. You have a lot of hates involved here tonight, Ralph. Why I mentioned two sides. I think they might have sent out for more of their crew. Busy mobiles.'

'Which hates?' Ralph replied.

'Gang hates. Crooked firms. Iles handling a revenge package for one of them, and for himself. He's assistant chief (Operations), isn't he? This is an operation. That's how they would see it – the others. Maybe he was paid. An inquiry will nose into that. Bank statements and so on. Possible laundering.'

'Iles wasn't there on the TV,' Ralph said.

'No, he wasn't, was he? Except we all know he was, don't we? And especially some of the people in here now know it. This is a character with a different name from Iles and a different appearance, because Ile's an actor and this is a telly drama. But underneath it's supposed to be the ACC, isn't it?'

This playing about with words such as 'know' infuriated Ralph. The tone was all wrong, in his view. Lecomte was here to pull pints and mix cocktails, not do clever-clever stuff about meanings – hark at him, the cheeky prick.

'The whole thing is about Iles, isn't it?'

True, of course, but Ralph detested the slickness of how Lecomte spoke it. Did he want to make Ralph sound naive and lumbering?

'Maybe I should do the same,' Lecomte said.

'Same as what?' Ralph asked.

'Get more people here to help us look after the place. I know some good lads. Help us stay in charge. I can text them. They'd be here fast. These are intelligent, restrained people, who know the human body and how to immobilize it. They'd do nothing more than is necessary, but what is necessary they'd do very nicely. Maybe a hundred quid each in cash for the night, and a few complimentary shorts when it's all over and they're about to leave – well-earned gratitude. We have to prevent news of a disturbance at The Monty spreading to the media. These boys could see to that. I've watched them manage it at other places where big violence started. But they need to kill the possibility off early, Ralph. I ought to give them a call. The strength of an army is its reserves, as we all understand. The club is lucky to have back-up very ready on call via, if I can say so, myself, Ralph.'

'Table four needs serving,' Ralph replied.

SIXTEEN

B eside that word 'know,' several others from this master-
mind potboy also offended Ralph.

Lecomte's pals would help 'us' look after 'the place',
apparently, if he let him summon them and dished out a few
hundreds. To Ralph, that 'us' made it sound like Lecomte
wasn't just a bit of hired lowlife on the club staff, but part-
owner with Ralph. God, the nerve! Now and then, or more
often, Lecomte seemed to believe in the aristocratic tinge of
his French first name – the count. Drop the 'o' and it might
be right.

Ralph considered Lecomte's cold reference to 'the place'
insulting for a potentially distinguished, chic, exclusive
Monty. The club hadn't quite made it to that point yet, but
Ralph had the progress under way. And then, beside the 'us'
there was a 'we'. 'We have to look after the place' and, 'We
have to prevent news of a disturbance spreading.' Here were
extra hints that Lecomte dreamed The Monty belonged to
both of them, and that he graciously accepted his share of
landlord responsibilities. There was even more than this.
Lecomte did seem to know of Ralph's devoted, evergreen
campaign to up the social standing of The Monty, and naturally
Lecomte in his delusion expected to be part of this triumph.
He fantasized about bringing in unnamed mates to head off an
outbreak of anarchy in the club, and so stop possible damaging
publicity about Monty lawlessness and non-resemblance to
The Athenaeum.

Lecomte had seemed to be thinking of a swift, possibly
brutal visit by his undainty associates who would then move
off to spend their fees. Ralph wondered about this. Lecomte
and his invited crew would be in possession of the club they
had just possibly saved from serious trashing. Ralph feared
they might feel they had conquerors' rights. Could they be
relied upon to leave? There was a song: 'We're here because

we're here because we're here because we're here'. No need for argument. Hitler said he marched into Czechoslovakia after Germans who lived there called for him to invade. It was an occupation, but disguised as something else. Likewise Lecomte and his little army at – in – The Monty? Lecomte obviously wanted the club. Was this the way to get it – Lecomte and his personal troop?

Lecomte took table four their drinks and then came back to stand alongside Ralph at his desk. The musicians were getting ready to play their final numbers.

'Do you carry something, Ralph?' Lecomte said, his tone extremely caring. 'I very sincerely hope you don't mind my inquiring, but over several weeks I've done a true scrutiny of your garments, including tonight's, but have been unable to detect anywhere a giveaway outline. However, I have to remember that you are the knowledgeable, perceptive type who would have your clothes tailored to disguise any such naff sign.'

Although Lecomte very sincerely hoped that Ralph wouldn't mind being gawped at in an eyes-only body search, Ralph *did* very sincerely mind, and minded quite a bit. When he chose his clothes, he wasn't thinking of how this twat would regard them week after week.

'Carry something?' Ralph replied.

'I know it runs against your thinking, but, well—'

'Against my thinking about what?' Ralph replied. He knew about what, of course, but wouldn't like Lecomte to imagine he and Ralph had any parallel ideas. Lecomte was pretentious enough already.

'Your views re. handguns in The Monty,' Lecomte replied. 'You're famous for not tolerating firearms on the premises, and this is very much to your credit; very, very much, it cannot be gainsaid but—'

'This is a social club, not a fucking shooting range,' Ralph said. 'Guns can have no part in The Monty's ambience.'

'I know that's how you individually feel, Ralph, and feel it with great conviction, but there are others who'd think and behave differently. That's why I wondered if you had something aboard ready – not to be used unprovoked. Oh, no, never unprovoked, I would not expect that of you, Ralph,' Lecomte had a kindly chuckle at the preposterous suggestion that Ralph might ever shoot first. 'There could be a simple, total need, though,' Lecomte said. 'No blame would attach to that, surely. As a very basic, elementary objective, we have to think of the fabric, don't we?'

'Do we? Which fabric?'

'Some of them might take against the TV screen because it seemed to glamorize Iles, depicting him as the noble and almost holy Avenger, sent among crooked empires with one purpose: cleansing.'

'How could it glamorize Iles? He wasn't there.'

'Some might not agree with that, Ralph. Result A: smash-it attack on the screen, which is why I said "fabric". And other fabric, too, such as upholstery of bench seats, panelling, the carpet. For no sensible reason, The Monty could become the focus of terrible ill-feeling, vivid, non-stop recriminations. People gripped by rage because of Iles have given up on sensible reasons. Things are calm now, but we can't count on that continuing, can we, Ralph?'

'Can't we? Everything feels very normal to me.'

This was a stark lie. It took Ralph a little while to work out what seemed unusual; and not just unusual, but unnerving. Ultimately, he came to think that maybe Lecomte had it right when he spoke of sides. He had meant two sides, one delighted by the way the murders were played in the television programme; the others hurt and enraged by it, and as a result dangerous. Although, Ralph didn't think things were as simple as that – not a straight division into a pair; there appeared to be a number of distinct, self-contained groups, some standing, a few at tables. Of course, there were always different bunches of friends and acquaintances at The Monty, that's how a club worked. But the degree of separation between the clusters struck Ralph as exceptionally strong tonight, as though some great gulfs were fixed. No interchange of people happened. They all seemed corralled with their clique of companions. Ralph thought that, say, three of these minor batches made up one of Lecomte's 'sides', and the three remaining formed the other.

Naturally, Ralph recognized some members in each of these small parties. He thought that if it came to trouble, he could guess which 'side' some of them would back. Members were allowed to sign in guests, though, on a twenty-four-hour licence, and there were several faces he did not know. They made it hard for Ralph to forecast what sort of fighting and vandalism might start.

He'd given Lecomte a brush-off session when he'd quizzed Ralph about armament, but now he thought he'd better get some fire power – a pity about the lines of his suit. He kept a couple of Walther automatics and a dozen rounds in his office safe. He stood and moved towards them. It was true that he banned guns from The Monty, but this didn't mean everyone obeyed and there could be occasions when Ralph might have to protect club members and himself. Acid, swords and sheath knives were also banned.

In private, he loaded one of the PK380 Walther models. His fingers were quick and steady. Although some people called him Panicking Ralph or Panicking Ralphy, in anything that concerned The Monty he was always totally strong and unshakable. It was as if his faith in the new Monty – the to-be Monty, the ideal, perfected Monty – was so powerful that it knitted some of this power into him physically. The owner of the forthcoming Monty would have courage, poise and dauntlessness as absolutely standard.

The cruel nicknames dated far back to a severe mess-up in a failed robbery. He didn't believe he had done anything weak and shameful there. In any case, that was a part of his life he'd almost forgotten, and kept trying to forget altogether. He was Ralph W. Ember, now, businessman, owner of a social club and a manor house, who had constructive, serious letters published in the press about environmental issues such as river pollution and fly-tipping.

The Walther would take eight rounds. Because he was so strict about guns in The Monty he put only four into the chamber. He realized this was absurd logic. Never mind, he liked to convince himself he had control and moderation, moderation that could be shelved if safety required.

He used a shoulder holster for the pistol. The Walther was

short barrelled and neat, designed for a concealed carry. All the same, Lecomte would certainly spot the bulge. Of course, he was right to say Ralph's suits were tailored personally for him, but they were cut to fit Ralph's normal measurements, not Ralph's measurements plus shooter and harness. Lecomte would gloat. He'd believe he had persuaded Ralph to tool up. And Ralph thought Lecomte possibly had. So sod him.

SEVENTEEN

I t wasn't exactly true that Jennifer Stippe-Lewis, one of the women hurt during the informalities at The Monty, had her chest crushed by a falling pool table. OK, Ralph would accept that she did have two or three broken ribs and it was the manhandled– menhandled – pool table that caused the injuries. But Jenny was not struck by its full weight, nor trapped underneath it among coloured balls from the table's smashed reservoir or pool, as some reports said.

Ralph thought it could reasonably be termed 'a glancing blow', but admittedly pool tables were lumpy objects and even a slight hit from one when off some of its stout legs could be serious. Although it was impossible to get accident insurance cover for The Monty, Ralph found that Jennifer had her own policy. There was a snag: the company queried her claim because underwriters could not visualize any ground-floor situation where a pool table might be in a position to fall on someone. This was not in the nature of pool tables. Jenny told him their argument was that normally people using the table would bend over it when playing their shots, so it was unlikely to be moving through the air like a punch or battering ram, capable of giving someone a bad knock at chest height. To ensure fairness in a pool game, the baize surface had to be absolutely steady and flat, the table firmly and evenly settled on the floor.

Ralph had seen the incident very late on that evening, and when he went to visit Jenny in hospital she asked if he would write a witness narrative for the insurer to back up her own account. Ralph wasn't sure now whether he had ever slept with Jenny, but he felt fond of her and wanted to help. He thought he remembered her being very fascinated by his face scar, stroking and primping it, but this was true of many women and it did not necessarily move on to something more. In any case, he felt a basic loyalty to quite a number of regular members of the club, men as well as women, particularly when something unfortunate had happened to them actually on Monty premises. Ralph would regard it as shallow and inhumane to offer sympathy only to those women members he'd unquestionably had it fully away with at least once.

But the idea of spilling all he knew about The Monty disturbance to the insurers made Ralph anxious. This was not the kind of club evening he would be happy to sketch for others. The insurers might promise confidentiality, but Ralph knew leaks leaked.

He had always loathed pool tables: American and vulgar, Ralph thought. But the membership wanted them. He would feel a real, undisguised contempt for the tables now. There'd be no pool in the new Monty.

Tone. That would be the crucial factor if he did write his version. He kept the word 'impulsive' very strongly in mind, ready for use. Obviously, he was bound to accept there had been something of a mishap. An outline of it would be in Jenny's original statement of claim. She was bound to see the facts from a very specialized, possibly unique, angle, though: on the end of wanton, wild violence from a pool table. But Ralph wondered whether the admittedly rough behaviour by some members could perhaps be explained as sudden flashes of temper and rage – yes, impulsive in a boisterous, maybe over-vigorous fashion, yet without any dark motive; mischievous, certainly, but not malevolent, and perhaps regretted very soon afterwards.

It wasn't a simple choice. He wanted the impetuous, hotheaded theme, but it would be stupid to make things sound trivial and of not much consequence. This might drastically weaken Jenny's case, cutting the possible payment or even stopping it altogether. He wished he could have studied her claim. She said she'd mentioned 'a considerable tension' at the club that night following a TV broadcast about two murders and its possible 'sly, oblique, damning' reference to a local police officer. This seemed to suggest that the flying pool table had something to do with a deeper matter: the aftermath of murder, murders.

Ralph regretted that she'd described the incident like that, and he'd have liked to see how she'd worded this part of her statement. She wouldn't have been thinking of how to protect The Monty's reputation. Her priority was to get good compensation. He didn't blame her for that. It was possibly an awkward detail, though.

Motive. This was the chief challenge for anyone dealing with the pool table episode. The insurers had aimed their questions at this mystery. How was it that six men decided to line themselves up along one side of the pool table then on 'three' in a 'one, two, three' preparatory jingle, crouch to take hold of the table's lower frame and lift it through an arc of 180 degrees until it fell front first near the bar, its stubby legs now pointed at the ceiling.

This semi-circle journey had produced the collision with Jennifer. She had been at the bar buying a couple of drinks, had turned to make her way back to her seat while carrying the glasses and was caught by the leading edge of the table as it swung towards its new upside-down anchorage, smashing her ribs and the glasses. The blow struck Jenny to the floor, but shoved her away from the table, so that she fell clear against the base of the bar on her back. This was why Ralph had thought of it as 'a glancing blow': the table did not fall on top of her but clipped Jenny as it passed.

Even so, it grieved Ralph that she could be savaged like that actually in a club owned by him, and of such rich, assured promise. Appalling. After the hospital visit he still had some of his uncertainties but eventually decided he must support her insurance claim. He'd do everything he could to apply maximum influence, and the influence of Ralph W. Ember was sometimes magical. He felt one way of fixing his problems might be to write out in full on the computer screen everything that had happened, including run-up and background, so it came over as absolutely authentic, convincing and strong, like the voice of Ralph W. Ember in person.

Then he'd methodically edit out all the bit, or bits, he thought potentially embarrassing and of no help to The Monty. Cutting was easy on the computer. He'd let the insurer have this nicely shortened scenario which would still contain some of the authenticity, convincingness and strength, but not foolishly too much.

EIGHTEEN

I am Ralph Wyverne Ember of Low Pastures, age forty-eight, proprietor of The Monty club at 11 Shield Terrace. I believe it necessary in the circumstances to give something of my background and civic standing. Of course, I do this not out of vanity, but so that you may know the status of someone ready to vouch for the integrity and truthfulness of Ms Jennifer Stippe-Lewis.

The club is renowned – not, I believe, too strong a term – as a community hub offering entertainment, social activities and constructive, vibrant local companionship. I think it fair to say that the club is already a prized asset in the city and, indeed, county; but it is also in a constant state of progressive development to keep pace with the changing requirements of our members.

I consider it a paramount duty to enhance The Monty's reputation and appeal by a sensitive programme of improvements, while at the same time maintaining the club's famed traditional appearance, personality and values. Some notion of the excellent relationship between the club and myself is an affectionate, amusing title awarded to me 'tongue in cheek' by members. It is 'M'Lord Monty'. This I must stress has no element of class distinction. I certainly don't regard myself as superior to quite a few members of The Monty. The nickname is simply a humorous expression of approval and respect. I am happy that Ms Jennifer Stippe-Lewis obviously feels that approval and respect and finds it natural and wise to seek my aid in this matter. I am delighted, indeed honoured, to provide it.

As with any worthwhile, stimulating club, a great range of opinion is represented in the membership, about the condition of the country, politics, cultural topics, education, crime prevention, fashion, soccer. Occasionally, this can lead to forceful arguments and sometimes even to violence, though violence of an unplanned, impulsive, short-lived kind. It was as an intensely regrettable incident during one of these outbursts that Ms Jennifer Stippe-Lewis, an esteemed, long-term Monty member, received injuries from an abnormally displaced club pool table. This was one of those deplorable, irresponsible acts in no regard aimed at Ms Jennifer Stippe-Lewis because of inflammatory views she'd expressed, but which by total mischance involved her receiving serious physical damage. This damage has been fully described, I know, in a report by doctors to you as insurers.

Let us ask, then, what was it that sparked the anger and disgraceful violence? My understanding is that a television broadcast shown on The Monty's large screen in the club bar started the unrest. How could this be in a club with such a fine reputation? The answer is not simple, but there is an answer, an answer with a consid-erable bearing on Ms Stippe-Lewis's claim.

The programme dealt with the murder of two criminals in an unsolved police case. This drama was presented as fiction, a piece of theatre rather than a documentary, but some groups in The Monty that night chose to take it as disguised fact, based on a strikingly similar local situ-ation – and not very well disguised. Attitudes among Monty members to the programme, and to its apparently real basis, varied greatly, and this led to outright conflict and vandalism.

What then were the main, fiercely opposed reactions to the broadcast that caused such appalling disorder?

(a) Some in the audience who thought they recognized an actual case behind the story-telling made it obvious they believed the two murdered criminals deserved their execution and thought the murderer a clever, God-given hero.

(b) But some of the murdered men's friends and rela-tives were also in the bar. I know now that they suspected the two had been killed by a high-ranking police officer. Several in this group apparently thought the investigation

*into the murders was deliberately cack-handed and inef-
fective because of the possible – probable – guilt of the
police officer. He could fix it that the investigation stalled
and stayed stalled.*

*At first, The Monty violence was shouts only. I cannot
report in full what was said because of libel and slander
risk. Here's a repeated yell, but edited: 'Nice one, ****,'
with the asterisks spelling out the name of a certain police
officer. Another chant was 'Crooked cop. Dirty double
killer', probably referring to the same officer but from
the reverse point of view. I saw that two battling factions
had formed.*

*The bellowing died away and fist-fighting started in
its place. This then worsened. Chairs and tall bar stools
were turned into weapons and missiles, fire extinguishers
activated and used like water cannons. I recognized
club members in both parties and it sickened me to see
something so contrary to the spirit of The Monty.*

*Jennifer had been to the bar to collect drinks. Some of
the fighting barred the way back to her table. She paused.
Near her, a group from one of the contingents suddenly
lined up alongside a pool table, lifted it and pushed it
over. Jennifer was standing with the drinks, looking for
a route across the room. She had begun to move, skirting
someone who was wildly using a rum bottle as a cosh.
This brought her close to the pool table, properly on its
legs at this stage, but then given this team shove. The
objective seemed to be isolation of enemies behind the
table, cornering them between the table and the outer
wall. Then they could be attacked and beaten up. But the
edge of the falling table caught Jennifer and knocked
her to the floor. She was in no way connected with either
party. It was an utterly random accident and, obviously,
subject of a totally justified personal injuries claim.*

R.W.E.

Ralph decided there would be absolutely no need to say in
his statement to the insurers that very untypically for him he'd
been carrying a gun. Perhaps a mention would have shown

that he'd expected difficulties at the club, and should have been ready to deal with them. But he told himself that insurers required a factual account of events, not a report on the state of Ralph's mind. They wanted to know what happened, not what he had feared might happen. Ralph felt sure they'd regard that as flim-flam – as waffle.

He didn't describe, either, how, not long after the fighting and violence had ended, Harpur and Iles had arrived at the club and viewed the destruction, though by then the pool table had been righted by the same team. Jennifer was on her way to hospital. Calls for an ambulance would always be passed on to the police, and Ralph saw he wasn't the only one to guess there could be reactions from a public showing of 'The Forgotten Murders'.

It was very late but Iles must have hung about the Control Room monitoring calls after watching the TV show where some would claim he starred. And if Iles hung about the Control Room he'd probably ring Harpur and get him out of bed when news about the club ruckus came through. That wouldn't worry Iles.

He was in uniform, the lights gleaming on his insignia, as if to register the return of nice behaviour and radiant decency. Ralph knew that to be laughable fraud, of course. After all, this was Iles.

He did a slow, bit-by-bit stare at the damage. 'Would you call it gratitude, Col?' he said.

'Which, sir?' Harpur replied.

'This splinterscape.'

'In what sense?' Harpur said.

Iles gave a small nod towards Ember's chest. 'Ralph takes aboard a shoulder harness and pistol yet does not use that pistol, despite the people who are set on carnage in his fine club who ought to have been shot. Are these slobs thankful? Are they fuck? Ralph restrains himself in that admirable style of his, which we knew about, but which we have never seen a more graphic example of.'

'It's only a blip,' Ralph said.

'What is?' Iles said.

'The disturbance.'

'A blip in which sense?' Harpur said.

'Col often asks about the sense of things, Ralph. He tries very hard to understand what's going on and it can be quite sad to watch the struggling, awkward effort.'

'I'll be improving The Monty very considerably,' Ralph replied.

'I've heard about that,' Iles said.

'I hope favourably,' Ember said.

'I've heard about it,' Iles said.

'You need a couple of Nobel prize winners among the membership,' Harpur said.

'That kind of thing,' Ralph said.

'They'll be queuing up,' Iles said.

'This is no real setback,' Ralph said.

'How could it be?' Iles said. But his voice was full of doubt and mockery. His voice generally *was* full of doubt and mockery when he spoke of Ember's hopes for The Monty. Sometimes Ralph put up with that. He and Mansel Shale had businesses that needed Iles's cooperation, so best not rile the sod. Occasionally, though, Ralph did do a bit of retaliation, but nothing too venomous.

'All that kind of unpleasantness will be eliminated then,' Ember said. 'And I'll make sure there are no fights over those two revenge murders, Mr Iles, one a very saucy but authentic garrotting. You, above all, don't want that kind of thing.'

'Which kind of thing?' Iles said.

'Scrapping. Destruction.'

'Why me above all?' Iles replied.

'Oh, yes,' Ralph said.

Ralph went behind the bar and got together some unbroken bottles and glasses on a tray. He mixed the usuals for Iles and Harpur – Iles's port and lemon, Harpur's gin and cider mix in a half-pint glass, and Ralph's own Kressmann Armagnac. Harpur found a serviceable table and some chairs. They sat among the wreckage with their drinks.

Iles took off his cap and put it on the table. 'I think I know what you have in mind when you talk of getting rid of unpleasantnesses in the club, Ralph,' he said.

'I expect you do,' Ember said.

'You mean a roving pool table,' Iles replied. 'That kind of item. The pool table is squatting there now all smug and primly settled but, you know, Ralph, that only a little while ago this very pool table flipped over in a completely non-pool-table fashion.'

'No, that isn't what I was getting at,' Ember said.

'Oh?' Iles said.

'I think I can see what's troubling Ralph,' Harpur said.

'You can, Col? *You* can?' Iles replied.

'It's to do with members of the club starkly divided about who killed the two crooks on TV,' Harpur said.

'But that's play-acting, fiction, isn't it, for God's sake?' Iles said.

'In a sense, sir, yes,' Harpur replied.

NINETEEN

On the whole, Harpur believed Iles did the killings, of course: the motive neatly there; Iles's turn-on rages always at the ready. Now and then Harpur found himself watching the ACC's hands and wondering whether they looked like a garrotter's, which Harpur thought might be lean, spidery, unforgiving. In fact, Iles's hands were stubby, a surprise on someone so slight. But he could probably adapt them to any kind of work as long as it interested him, and garrotting was the kind of work that *would* interest him. Iles's interests were remarkably wide, not all of them destructive.

Because it was Iles – was almost certainly Iles who saw off the pair – there would be a stout, sweetly constructed wall against detection. It was not a matter of deliberately messing up the investigation, obstructing it as self-security, though Harpur realized some powerful figures believed this and might get intrusive and foully painstaking.

He could have told them, but didn't, that attempts at detection foundered because Iles knew before he began how to make sure there was nothing for an investigation to fix on, feed on. After all, he was assistant chief constable (Operations). Almost mystical skill and ruthless drive shone in most of his operations, but several of his others lay in lovingly contrived, dense darkness. Although the doomed nature of the investigation itself offered evidence that this was an Ilesian job, it was not the kind of evidence leading to jail. *'My lord, I present a case where the failure to convict is irresistible proof that the accused should be convicted.'*

The Times and *Daily Telegraph* published reviews by their television critics of 'The Forgotten Murders', and later in the day the giveaway local *Evening Bulletin* had a report of the violence at The Monty. Harpur thought that between them the three gave a convincing sketch of things, and he wished they didn't. 'The Forgotten Murders' itself was almost certain to create what might turn out to be unwanted Home Office nosiness. The press involvement was likely to increase and sharpen it.

Denise had run out of cigarettes and got up early to go to the corner shop. Also she wanted to see what the papers made of 'The Forgotten Murders' and she came back with copies of the two nationals. Their critics would have been given an advance showing of the programme.

Denise took off her jeans and got back into bed. Hazel and Jill must have heard her go out to the shop and came into the bedroom now with mugs of tea for her and Harpur. The girls sat on each side of the foot of the bed. Denise lit up a cigarette and took a couple of deep, soul-refreshing pulls. She placed the cigarette on the bedside ashtray, drank some tea, put the mug on the floor and opened the *Telegraph* to the critic's column. She read silently for a couple of minutes. Then she said: 'There's someone called Prunella.'

'Called what?' Jill said.

Denise read aloud now: '"Last night's drama spot offering 'The Forgotten Murders' raised, in her nuanced but provocative style, director Prunella Gart's version (script by Arnold Bourne) of the occasional resounding clash between legality and so-called natural justice. It traced with admirable thoroughness and unwavering narrative force the kind of dilemma that has challenged philosophers, lawyers and theologians for centuries."'

'"Nuanced"?' Jill said. 'What's that?'

'Subtle changes of meaning or tone,' Hazel replied.

'Norman Mailer said newspapers crush nuances like nuts,' Denise said.

'It's a good thing, is it?' Jill said.

'What?' Hazel replied.

'To be nuanced,' Jill said.

'But also provocative,' Hazel said. 'One bit nice and gentle, the next a smack in the chops.' She unfolded *The Times* on the bed.

Denise read aloud from the *Telegraph* again. '"The problem confronted so skilfully here is easy to summarize but not to solve: If the police and courts are obviously failing to safeguard the public and stamp out evil, can someone, or more than one, legitimately assume those protection and punishment duties personally? Treatments of this theme take plenty of forms."'

Denise reclaimed the burning cigarette and took in another stalwart helping of fume. Harpur, still lying flat in the bed, eyes closed, holding the tea mug in one hand, said: 'We're talking kangaroo courts and vigilantes, aren't we?'

'Kangaroo?' Jill said.

'Courts with no genuine legal status, and possibly vindictive,' Hazel said.

'It's what *The Godfather* films are about,' Denise said. 'Italian immigrants in the United States at the start of the last century found they couldn't trust the police to look after them and so they set up their own law-and-order structure under a gang supremo.'

'*The Times* says there's a novel and film called *The Caine Mutiny* which asks whether a warship's officers are right to take over if the captain seems cowardly and mad,' Hazel replied.

'Bogart as the cracked captain,' Denise said, 'scared of almost everything and with overworked worry beads.' She finished her cigarette and began to read again: '"Although 'The Forgotten Murders' is by no means the first to explore the topic, Prunella Gart brought a new wit, depth, pace and credibility to this chewy moral puzzle. In 'The Forgotten Murders', a police chief hunting for evidence to nail a tycoon drugs dealer sends one of his young detectives undercover to get more information on the crooked businessman. This operation is botched, though, with the spy exposed and slaughtered. The drugs lord and an accomplice are arrested and accused of the killing but get off. The officer who devised the operation is distraught over his detective's death, and then at the acquittal.

'"And so, he carries out a mock-judicial execution of the pair himself. Or does he? Although 'The Forgotten Murders' ends with heavy hints that he does, the conclusion is not totally clear."'

Hazel said: '*The Times* thinks some of its readers will regard this as evasive, "a cop cop-out," but that "the careful imprecision and reasonable bafflement are in splendid harmony with the general ambience of what has gone before." Then we get back-slapping for the actors: "Hugh Phareas as the heart-broken, vengeful officer is excellently sinuous, emotionally powerful, calculatedly defiant of rules and precepts. Trevor Lichen gives the drugs baron occasional moments of human and humane feeling, but doesn't overdo it.'"

Harpur spent most of the rest of the day in his office at headquarters. The Press Bureau sent a clipping up to him from the *Evening Bulletin*.

> *A woman was rushed to hospital last night following an outbreak of fighting and vandalism at one of the city's best-known social clubs, The Monty in Shield Terrace. Furniture, shelving, glassware and a large-screen television set were wrecked during a fifteen-minute period of turmoil. The smashing of the television screen was believed to have a special significance.*
>
> *Jennifer Steppe-Lewis, aged 32 of Mildmay Avenue, was struck in an exceptional accident with an ungrounded pool table and suffered serious injuries to her chest. Rioters grabbed spirits and wine bottles from behind the bar and swigged the contents, causing the spread of drunkenness and increased violence. The proprietor of the club was present, but unable to control the outburst.*
>
> *Police arrived at the club later. They included Assistant Chief Constable Desmond Iles and Detective Chief Superintendent Colin Harpur. The presence of such senior officers would suggest the disturbance had some special, so-far-undisclosed, significance.*
>
> *The violence apparently began after a showing of the TV programme, 'The Forgotten Murders'. Different parts of this 'faction' item – a mixture of documentary and drama – appeared to raise anger and resentment in varying groups of the members and caused them to attack each other.*
>
> *Mr Ralph W. Ember, owner of The Monty said: 'This violence was disgraceful and entirely untypical of the club.' He said that 'outside elements' appeared to be among the attackers. He seemed to think that the trouble*

had been pre-planned by people who regarded The Monty as a suitable site for their display of 'arrant power'.

'I do not know what led to the terrible behaviour but people may rest assured that I will not let it happen again. The club is temporarily closed while repairs are carried out but we expect to reopen with everything back to normal by 6 p.m. We all hope that Jennifer Steppe-Lewis, one of our most valued members, will make a good and quick recovery.'

Asked whether the involvement of two very high-rank police officers indicated some unusually grave concern about the incident, Mr Ember said he was grateful for their visit but did not know of any unusual interest in the very regrettable occurrence. Mr Ember said he would vigorously continue a scheme already under way to enhance the existing strong appeal of The Monty and would not be deterred by 'this or any other unfortunate blips.'

Iles came in while Harpur was reading the *Bulletin*'s report. He was in shirt sleeves and looked frail and boyish. He wasn't. 'Brilliant, isn't it, Col?' he said. A beautiful smile had taken over his face.

'What, sir?'

'I adore the way they pair our names – Assistant Chief Constable Desmond Iles (Operations) and Detective Chief Superintendent Colin Harpur.'

'Journalists like to get names correct.'

'The reporter says for us to be at The Monty must indicate something "special" and "grave". It needed someone of high rank to deal with it – myself. But they mention you as well, a kind of linkage. It helps give me the common touch, the very common touch. That can be important in police work.'

'But what makes it special and grave, sir?'

'Have you ever heard of a pool table assaulting a woman before?' Iles replied.

'That's a point, sir.'

TWENTY

Mansel Shale appeared at The Monty for a talk with Ralph not long after repairs and replacements had been completed. The club was running normally again and Ember felt joyful relief. The appalling damage done in that spell of havoc had brought him deep suffering as though he'd been injured himself, although, in fact, he was unhurt. His hopes for The Monty had seemed shattered. But those hopes were too powerful to fade. They'd soon resumed.

Mansel wore navy Lycra long shorts and a silver top, red striped training shoes and a turquoise chin-strapped helmet. Ralph had never seen him in this kind of outfit before and would have preferred not to see him in it now, but he couldn't say so to Mansel: it would be cruel. Shale had a 1930s-style bicycle with Sturmey-Archer hub gears and completely encased chain. He had ridden over from his home in the ex-St James's rectory on the other side of the city. It was just after midday. Ralph usually came in around eleven a.m. to make sure the club was ready for business. He believed in being very 'hands-on', especially now following the flare-up. Shale took off the helmet and hung it on the bike's handlebars. He put the machine into the club cloakroom and Ralph led him to his office on the first floor.

Mansel wasn't a regular at The Monty and Ralph guessed the visit could mean something special. There were a couple of armchairs in the office and they sat facing each other. Ralph rang down to the kitchen and asked for coffees to be brought up. Mansel said: 'As a matter of fact, Ralph, I got pictures and pictures can be all very terrific, no question, in what might be described as the realm of the visual, but they're all the better if we can give them some reality also, which is why I said to myself, "Go to The Monty and see the shape and size of things in what we might call situ", which means being there, solid and three-dimensional in their proper place.'

'You're always welcome at the club, Manse,' Ember said, even when you're in that sickening gear – but Ralph only thought the last bit, didn't actually say it.

'This I know and am grateful for. But what we need, in my opinion, Ralph, is the geography of certain incidents,' Shale replied. 'Geography in a so-to-speak way, not rivulets or abysses but the inside of The Monty.'

'To what purpose, Manse?' Ralph said.

'Truth,' Shale said.

'Truth as to what?'

'Truth. Identification. These I believe you'll agree are important.'

Well, yes, Ralph thought he might agree, if he knew what the fuck Manse was talking about. 'Truth in which aspect?' Ember asked. 'Whose identification?'

'You're certainly entitled to ask such questions,' Shale replied. 'I recognize there is some lack of clarity so far.'

'Thank you, Manse.'

'I got pictures on my phone and they definitely tell a tale, but that tale will be so much clearer when we have got the actual setting such as chairs, the bar, the bottles, the pool table. That pool table is very, very real or it would not be able to cuff a woman's tits to the point of hospitalization.'

'We've got everything back to as it should be,' Ember replied.

'You have indeed, Ralph, and it's what I would expect. This is a club with a glorious, wide reputation, and that reputation had to be worked for, and still has to be if you are to keep that reputation, and, yes, even improve on it. When I read about the rotten trouble here, such as the pool table and multi-breakages, I decided I must come to The Monty and bring support, to a good friend and trade colleague.'

'Thanks, Manse.'

'Of course, you were there at the time,' Mansel said.

'Yes.'

'Distressing.'

'Yes, distressing.' That was on the way to being the right sort of word, but nothing like strong enough. He had felt appalled and helpless. He'd had the gun aboard after Lecomte's persuasion, and, of course, there'd been a previous gun conversation with Mansel over at the rectory, but a gun wouldn't have been of any use at the Monty trashing. He didn't bring it out of the holster. He couldn't simply fire into a mob. The gun was in case he needed to protect himself, not to wound and possibly slaughter willy-nilly on Monty premises.

'You'll have a general idea of what went on,' Mansel said.

'How do you mean, Manse – "general"?'

'Disruption on all sides and up the middle.'

'Yes. It seemed to be about some TV programme that had been on earlier, before I arrived.'

'You wouldn't see any pattern to it all, just violence everywhere, Ralph. Disgraceful.'

'Pattern?'

'The photos might show us that pattern.'

'What pattern?'

'Which is why they are useful, maybe.'

'But in what way?'

'This support I think I can offer is in two forms, Ralph,' Shale replied. 'First, to ask around and try to find anyone who was in the club that night and might of took photos of the behaviour on their phone. This is how matters are today, isn't it, Ralph – people don't believe something has happened unless they can take a pic of it? Second, when I discovered, yes, there are folk with such pictures, to get a look at them pictures, copy them, and see how they fit the layout of the club interior, and match the pictures with the reality of that roughhouse time. And so we got a background or what we might call a setting.

'A context?'

'That sort of thing I expect,' Shale said. 'We know for certain.'

'What, Manse?'

'Oh, yes, for certain.'

'You sound very confident.'

'A face,' Mansel replied.

'Whose?'

'It appears, reappears. But we have a background for it and a what-you-call, like you said.'

'Context.'

'Right. We've spoke before regarding the possible need to do someone, haven't we, Ralph, the aim to protect Ilesy and therefore protect our well-being.'

'Certainly.'

'But no movement.'

'Not yet.'

'No, not yet,' Manse replied. 'But now comes something that could really help things along.'

'Yes?'

'Oh, yes indeed. I want you to look at these pics and notice a face, one face, a face that's very, very present during that Monty disturbance. Behind the face in these photos there are always items we recognize because they belong to The Monty – the bar, chairs and tables, broken or not, the pool table legs in the air at that juncture but now properly restored. The face is there among them, all completely genuine. These pics are not faked. They can't be faked because we have the genuine what-you-call for them.'

'Context.'

'Right. This is why I say a pattern, Ralph.'

'How do you mean, a pattern, Manse?'

'The pattern becomes obvious because we are looking at the scene not just once or twice but in a load of instances.' Manse held out his phone and rolled about a dozen pictures of the Monty devastation for Ralph to examine. It wasn't what Ember really wanted to see and to be reminded of, but Mansel seemed to believe something crucial was there. 'Do you spot it?' he asked.

'What?'

'The face.'

Ember squinted hard at the pictures as Shale kept them on the move.

'Well, yes, perhaps,' Ralph said.

'This is not a "perhaps". This is a certainty. This is a face in a context. This face and this context are the truth, Ralph.'

'Hold it,' Ember replied.

Mansel stopped scrolling the pictures.

'Up here, to the left?' Ralph said, pointing a finger. 'That the one?' He didn't think he'd noticed this face during the actual outbreak. It wasn't someone he recognized. And Mansel was probably right to say that there was too much going on for Ralph to register any 'pattern' in those minutes of chaos.

Now, in Ralph's office, Mansel gave three big, pleased nods. Ember thought they were the kind of showy nods that were just right for someone in Lycra long shorts. 'Well done, Ralph. Yes, that's our boy.' Shale flicked through a couple more pictures. 'Here he is again, you see, Ralph? He's standing near a heap of broken glass and waving his arm about.'

'Yes,' Ember said.

'Or here again,' Shale said, as the pictures shifted. 'It's clear in this one he's not just waving an arm, he's throwing a punch, and in the next one somebody on the floor near him, caught by that haymaker fist I'd say and knocked flat, such brutality so wrong for the spirit and the soul of The Monty. Who is he?'

'Who? The man on the floor?' Ember said.

'No. The face.'

'You don't recognize?'

'Should I? It's why I mentioned identification,' Manse said.

'You know him?'

'I didn't. I asked around,' Manse said. 'Name, address. He's got some fame. What we have here is what I would regard as an example – the destruction, the arm waving, the punch.'

'An example of what, Manse?'

'An example of the whole situation. It tells us what that whole situation is, like typical, like summing it all up in one go, a sort of what-you-call . . . not context but . . . like that musical instrument.'

'Symbol, but with an S and an O not a C and an A, like for the instrument.'

'Yes, a symbol, standing for much more than itself only.'

As always with Manse there was a vivid, inspiring liveliness to his features. Ralph thought he looked like a very well-connected ferret. He glowed now, obviously delighted that Ralph had found his way to this possibly key face.

'The name is Favard,' Shale said.

'Ah,' Ember replied.

'Yes, it's worth an "Ah", isn't it, Ralph?'

'Ah,' Ralph said.

'Of the two deads in the unsolved murders case, one, I think, was called Favard, wasn't he?'

'Paul Favard.'

'This one – the ever-present pictured face – is Naunton (Waistcoat) Favard, a brother of Paul. It's what I mentioned previous, Ralph.'

'What?'

'Identification. Among the shambles and confusion in The Monty on that bad, bad night, there is this constant, strong face on view in the middle of things, as if it wanted to tell us what it's all about. It's a symbol with an S and an O. But no need for him to tell us. We know, don't we, Ralph?'

'Perhaps.'

'Oh, there's that "perhaps" again,' Mansel said. It was half laugh, half snarl. 'So cagey, Ralph, so undecided. But it's absolutely plain, isn't it? This is a Favard to avenge a Favard, isn't it? This one comes from away, but is very much part of the crooked family. A Favard – Waistcoat Favard – doesn't like how the telly treated the Favard story. The name of the dead character in the programme wasn't Favard, of course: a different safety-first identification, but behind this little bit of writer's trickery it's no question the late Paul.'

One of the barmen came in with a coffee pot on a tray, hot milk in a jug, a sugar bowl and two cups and saucers. He left and Ralph poured. Mansel added milk and a couple of sugar lumps. Ralph took his black, no sugar. Shale said: 'This is why I think it's all to do with identity and identification, Ralph. First, identify the place. Well, that's easy, it's The Monty. We got pics that show us the location, but even without the pictures we'd most likely know it was The Monty because The Monty is such a great centre for the community, so loved by the community. The Monty is like a kindly mirror of everything important that happens in that community. For this, Ralph, you deserve major, non-stinting-type praise.'

'Thank you, Manse.'

'So we got an identity for the location and then we ask what the violence in that location was *re*. – we identify it.

And here's the answer, Ralph: it was to do with them two deads, Favard and the other, plus also relating to Assistant Chief Constable (Operations) Desmond Iles – or whatever he was called in the telly stuff. That's the identification, Ralph. That's the bigger, vital background, known also as a context.'

He drank his coffee slowly, all of it. This seemed to Ralph a very decisive way of drinking coffee. It revealed outright mastery over what had been in the cup. It was gone in one short series of swallows, Mansel's. He stood. Ralph had been about to pour him a refill. He saw now, though, that this would cheapen the way Mansel had dealt with the first: that dignified and resolute style could not be cloned. 'I'd like to go down, Ralph,' Shale said.

'Down where?'

'Down to where it was,' Manse said.

'Where what was?'

'The fighting, the destruction, the perilously unfixed pool table, the punch.'

There was no dress code for The Monty, though Ralph would definitely install one when he'd raised the club to a higher level socially. Even now, though, he didn't fancy having Mansel around the bar in those shorts. They were probably fine for cycling, but not at all for the club. Early drinkers below would be shocked to see someone in that kind of glinting ensemble. Of course, they knew that cyclists wore shorts, but cyclists didn't generally wear them in The Monty: wrong tone.

TWENTY-ONE

B ut Ralph went down with Mansel to the bar, and at once
Shale placed himself in what he must regard as the position Naunton (Waistcoat) Favard had during the violence.
Mansel was fond of actuality, or at least something very close
to it. He kept his phone in one hand and consulted it now and
then, like someone with a sextant, so he could work out what
he'd termed the 'geography' of things. When he'd settled
at the selected point he glanced at Ralph, plainly wanting him
to confirm the choice. Manse required total authenticity for
his make-believe. Ember nodded, not an extravagant series of
rocking-horse nods like Shale's when they were talking in the
office, and only a single, slight nod, but decisive.

The din of the outbreak had come with the photos: sounds
of smashing, splintering, shattering, pulverizing, cracking.
And shouting, but Ralph could make out only the occasional
word, no joined-up phrase or sentence with a meaning:
'riddance', 'corrupt', 'fucking', 'plot', the 'fucking' four times
but only as a curse.

From his fancied situation near a heap of smashed bottles
and glasses, Mansel slowly, systematically eye-balled the
imagined, scrapping crowd, at first waving an arm at them
and then letting go with a swinging right upper-cut to a fantasy
jaw. Ralph thought the sequence nearly balletic.

Although it was only just after midday, early for a club,
the bar already had some customers. Tim (Tasteful) Barry-
Longville sat with Mavis, his mother, at a replacement table
in their usual sector of the room. They sometimes came in
for a pre-lunch drink. 'You're looking so svelte in that rig,
Mansel,' Tasteful called.

'But he's not supposed to be Mansel, is he,' his mother said.
'He's the one they call "Waistcoat", yes. Ralph? A Favard.
He was yelling about a fucking shameless fucking corrupt
cop plot to hide the fucking murder of his brother, Paul, and

someone else.' She and Tasteful must have been nearer to
Waistcoat on the night and able to hear him properly.

'We love the way you felled that laddie who'd been
screaming, "Good riddance to Paul Favard and the other . . ."
the other . . . how did it go, Ma?' Tasteful said.

'"The other fucking creep. Three cheers for do-it-yourself
Ilesy,"' Mavis said. She had on khaki linen trousers and a
man-style brown, yellow, beige check shirt and red cravat.
Tasteful was in one of his three-piece suits, a white rose in
the buttonhole.

'Then Waistcoat Favard floored him,' Tasteful said.
'Brotherly love for dead Paul Favard.'

'Not Favard in the programme,' Mavis said.

'The one who was meant to be Paul Favard in the
programme,' Tasteful said. 'A victim.'

'We don't know who he was meant to be,' Ralph replied.

'Of course we do,' Mavis said. She leaned forward and
pointed at the shoulder of Ember's jacket. 'I see you're
carrying a pistol, Ralph. Did you have it with you during the
rough stuff? Weren't you tempted to use it?'

'Ralph's not like that, Mother. He's got a humane, moral
side,' Tasteful said.

'He has?' Mavis said. 'Sounds like an encumbrance for
somebody in his kind of game, or games.'

Ember went with Mansel to the cloakroom for his bike
and waited while he refitted the helmet.

'They're probably right, don't you think, Ralph?' Shale said.

'Tasteful and Mave? Right about what?'

'You,' Shale said.

'What about me?'

'Too tender,' Shale said.

'Who to?'

'It's obvious.'

'What is?'

Manse wheeled the cycle towards the main door of the
club. 'I used to think we ought to remove any investigator
who came here from London touting for dirt on Des Iles,' he
said. 'But that could be too late. If someone was sent by
Whitehall to poke about into the past it would mean the hunting

was already under way and Iles is in peril. What we got to do, Ralph, is stop anyone like that before he even starts. Or she. The priority job is to get rid of someone like Waistcoat who's yelling these insults and filthy slanders about Desy Iles and causing very unnecessary, foul attention to them deaths. Correction: not someone *like* Waistcoat, *but* Waistcoat. He's got to be removed, Ralph.'

'Removed?'

'It's what Mavis said. You could of done him that bad night and you would of had an excuse for it, like justifiable – the sod a chief wrecker of your beautiful, bonny, brain-child Monty. But you're one with complicated feelings, such as sensitivity and kindliness, always have been, Ralph. It's your personal nature and can't be helped. I understand why you didn't shoot. I don't feel no blame toward you or anything like that. In a different kind of world them qualities of yours might be just what was wanted, leading to an MBE or similar. So, Waistcoat is still around with his mouth and his brother-based hate, definitely, but he shouldn't be *definitely*.'

Ember said: 'Manse, it's best at this stage to—'

But Shale pushed the bike ahead of him across the pavement, swung his leg over the saddle and joined the Shield Terrace traffic.

TWENTY-TWO

'Hazel's gone.' Louder: 'Col, she says Hazel's gone.' Harpur always came out of sleep more slowly than Denise. He reckoned unconsciousness had a lot to be said for it. 'What?' He opened his eyes.

'Jill says Hazel's gone.'

'Gone?' Harpur grunted. 'Where?' It was another of those bedroom visits, but this time only Jill. She stood at the foot of the bed in her dressing gown, the door open and the landing light on behind her. Harpur thought she looked jubilant. The bedside clock showed 1.17 a.m.

'I heard something and went to look but she wasn't there,' Jill said.

'Heard what?' Harpur had almost reached full awareness and realized he sounded like an interrogation. He sat up in bed alongside Denise, softened his voice and sweetened the phrasing: 'You thought you heard something, did you, love?'

'Not thought, did,' Jill replied.

'And was it something in the house?' Harpur said.

'Most likely in the house,' Jill said.

'What kind of sound?' Harpur said.

'A sound like a sound,' Jill replied. 'So I went and knocked on her bedroom door. That made a sound, but a different kind of sound – like someone knocking a door.'

'Yes?' Harpur said.

'Usually, I wouldn't knock, just walk in, but . . . well, it was so late.'

'OK,' Harpur said.

'But no answer,' Jill said.

'No?' Harpur said. 'Hazel asleep?'

'So I opened the door and called her name,' Jill said.

'I thought I heard something,' Denise said. 'You must have woken me, Jill.'

'Her bedroom light wasn't on,' Jill said.

'Hazel not in her bed?' Harpur said.

'At first I thought she was,' Jill said. 'The duvet wasn't flat; it had like a lumpiness under it.'

'But?' Denise said.

'I went into her room, and I think I called her name again.'

'But still no answer?' Harpur said.

'Then I could see it was a pillow,' Jill said.

'Deliberately to make it look as if she was still there?' Denise said.

'Like in some of those old films on The Movie Channel,' Jill said. 'About boarding schools, so a kid wouldn't be missed if he or she did a flit from the dorm. That's what it's called in boarding schools, "the dorm", where they sleep, meaning dormitory. I went and got my mobile phone and called her number. It rang in the wardrobe. She hadn't taken it.'

'Forgotten?' Harpur said.

'Hazel never forgets her phone,' Jill said.

'She was afraid she could be traced – located – through it,' Denise said.

Or if she'd been snatched she might not have had time to pick it up. This was another of those thoughts Harpur did not speak. 'Have you checked the bathroom?' he said.

'Dark. Nobody there,' Jill said. She gave a massive grin. Happy excitement suddenly flooded her voice. 'Do you think she's what's known as eloped, Dad?'

'Eloped?' Harpur said.

'Scarpered because of very seriously forbidden love,' Jill said. 'The people who do it don't bother about a wedding dress and posies.'

'Which people?' Harpur said.

'Couples who elope. I've read about it. When the bride is very young or very rich or both. They used to run away to Scotland because up there people didn't worry about the details. Often a pair would do a runner in the middle of the night. They didn't care what people thought. They had to be together because of fierce love. They wouldn't brook any opposition. I came across that word "brook" meaning not a stream but put up with.'

'Her clothes gone?' Harpur said.

'She's been very worried about Desy Iles,' Jill replied.

'Worried why?' Harpur said.

'Oh, you know, Dad,' Jill said. 'He used to act very sweet on her. He had a crimson scarf he used to wear loose, so he'd seem sort of romantic and dashing and less old.'

'That finished,' Harpur said.

'But she still, well . . . she thinks about him, if you know what I mean, Dad. And some of the kids at school said the telly play the other night was really about him. And a big row about him took place in a club. One of the kid's fathers is an odd-job man and had to do emergency repairs there.'

'Finished,' Harpur replied.

'It wasn't just the scarf,' Jill said.

'Finished,' Harpur said.

'Maybe, Dad. But she found out people were trying to get him.'

'How do you mean, "get him"?' Denise said.

'Get him,' Jill replied.

'Get him for what?' Denise said.

'Yes, for what, Jill?' Harpur said.

'Like for those two murders on TV, although all the names were different. They could not have a drama with someone called Assistant Chief Constable (Operations) Desmond Iles because that would be what's referred to as libel, and Desy could sue them for saying he was a multi-murderer, although an assistant chief. That drama is like them parables in the Bible – it says more than just the story. Yes, Haze thinks of him a lot. She doesn't talk to me about this because it's private. But I can tell. Maybe they've escaped – not to Scotland because Mr Iles is already married, but done a bunk to somewhere secret, perhaps abroad in a country where they understand about love boiling over and that kind of thing, and don't know about the murders.'

Denise got out of bed. She had on joke pyjamas, khaki with big silver broad arrows the way prison clothes used to be. 'Let's see if there's a note somewhere shall we, Jill?' she said. 'And your dad can get dressed.'

'Do you think it was Iles, Denise?' Jill asked.

'What?' Denise said.

'Who did those two. Dad won't say yes or no because he's police. They keep quiet until they can tell the jury exactly what they want the jury to hear.'

'We'll have a search,' Denise replied.

'In some ways it's all lovely, isn't it?' Jill said. 'If she and Des have gone, but then you got to wonder whether she'd want to be on her own in quite, well . . . *personal* conditions with a killer? Haze can be very particular. And Des is Operations. Who'd see to all that? He couldn't keep ringing up from Greece or Tasmania to give orders to the Control Room.'

She went with Denise to take a more thorough look at Hazel's room. Harpur put some clothes on and then did a quick inspection of the rest of the house. He discovered nothing unusual, no note from Hazel, no signs that anyone had broken in and possibly taken her away. A denim jacket she occasionally used was in its place on the hall coat-hanger.

Denise joined Harpur downstairs. She'd persuaded Jill to go back to bed. Denise had pulled a sweater and jeans on over her pyjamas. She had a cigarette half smoked in the side of her mouth. Harpur's Ford was parked in front of the house. He took a long look both ways in Arthur Street but saw no movement. They got into the car. Harpur said: 'I'll drive slowly. Can you watch for someone walking, possibly with a haversack on her back, Denise? Or perhaps riding a bike.'

'Where are we going?' she said.

'Rougemont Place.'

'What's Rougemont Place?' she said.

'Expensive housing. Iles lives there. A house called Idylls.'

'Tennyson,' Denise replied.

'Most probably.'

'*Idylls of the King*,' Denise said. 'A collection of poems.'

'Suits. He's a Tennyson fan. Likes what he calls his "bigness".'

'Maybe too big.'

'Yes?'

'"Break, break, break,/On thy cold grey stones, O Sea!/ And I would that my tongue could utter/The thoughts that arise in me."'

Harpur said: 'Iles never had any trouble uttering the thoughts that arose in him, especially the brutal and/or snotty ones.'

'We changed it at school.' Denise said:

'"Cake, cake, cake,/Oh those cold grey scones for tea?/I'd rather have tongue and trotter,/True grub for a girl like me."'

'Of course, three or four streets can lead to Rougemont. We don't know which she might take,' Harpur replied.

'You believe what Jill said?'

'Which?'

'Eloping.'

'Of course not.'

'So why are we going to Rougemont?'

'I don't believe it, you don't believe it, but Hazel might see things differently. This is a kid under stress. We can't be sure how she'll behave. Perhaps she hopes to show Iles that not everyone is against him. Is she trying to prove she'll stand by him regardless?'

'Been on a child psychology course lately, Colin?' Denise said. 'Do you think she's going to ring his front door bell in the middle of the night and invite him to a new life somewhere? His wife is at home, isn't she, and a child?'

'She might be pregnant. I don't know what Hazel will do. And I don't know what to do myself. I can't ring up the Control Room and ask if they've had sightings of a teenager trudging alone through the city. I'm a detective chief super-intendent. Do I want to broadcast that I've got a deeply troubled daughter, maybe linked somehow to the ACC?'

'Poor Colin,' Denise replied. She leaned across and patted his arm.

'Stay alert,' he said. 'Maybe we'll find her before she does anything crazy.' He realized this assumed she still had charge of herself. That could be untrue. What had happened, and what was happening, might have nothing to do with Iles and a schoolgirl crush. Denise must be thinking the same. Harpur had enemies. He tried to shut out the idea. Tact and kindness kept Denise silent on this, too.

After a while with no sighting of Hazel, Harpur said: 'You're probably right, Denise, and we're on a useless trek. This has knocked me silly – the thoroughness of the planning.'

'Hazel is very sensible,' Denise said.

'She is, and she's turned it against us,' Harpur said. 'Most of the evidence seems to show she had arranged the exit herself. Some anxiety, some intent, must have been building in her for a while and I didn't notice.'

'Is she on the pill, Colin?'

'She's only fifteen.'

'Some doctors wouldn't quibble.'

Of course, Harpur knew this. He'd wondered. It was as far as he'd go. If she'd wanted him to know she'd tell him. That's how Hazel was. She too had a right to silence. As he prepared for a prowl around Idylls he thought it strange that Sarah Iles had come to his house in Arthur Street looking for possible information about her husband, and now Harpur wanted a look at her home for possible information about his daughter and the assistant chief.

They had reached Rougemont Place and not found Hazel. Iles's house showed no lights. Harpur left the car and did a swift prowl in the garden of Idylls, finishing at the front door. Useless. He had to keep his survey short. Householders in this kind of neighbourhood would be sensitive about a figure apparently casing one of the properties at two a.m. Someone up for a pee might glance from a bedroom window – might, in fact, call the police. Harpur didn't fancy having to explain to a patrol why he was giving the ACC's villa the once-over.

When he returned to the car, Denise said: 'Colin, I've been thinking.'

'I rely on you for that.' It sounded jokey but wasn't. He did value her brain. It sometimes helped her dismantle a problem faster than his. And this wasn't a jokey situation, anyway – a child missing.

'That club Jill was talking about,' Denise said.

'The Monty.'

'I'd heard the same sort of reports.'

'Which? 'Harpur said.

'To do with the TV thing, saying more than it seemed to. I wondered whether Hazel might decide there'd be insights on Iles at the club. She'd heard about the TV fracas.'

'Almost everyone has heard of it,' Harpur said.

'But for her it's special.'

'Maybe.'

'So I mobiled Directory for their number and rang them. They were just closing. I did the lost kid bit and asked the woman who answered whether she'd seen anything of a girl too young for The Monty but asking a lot of questions. She said the club owner – Mr Ember – on one of his outdoor security checks of the building saw a teenager arguing with two of the bouncers and went to find what it was about. The woman didn't know the outcome except that Mr Ember had sent the girl home with a chaperone by taxi.'

TWENTY-THREE

Two points from Ralph's past:
(a) He knew a couple of hitmen;
(b) He also knew how difficult and anxious teenage daughters could be.

He didn't really like the term, hitmen. It seemed crude and overdramatic. The hitmen he'd met, back a few years now, and well before The Monty era, didn't regard hits as a vocation, like priesthood or nursing. Hardly ever was it their main career and exclusive income source, only an occasional freelance sideline. They'd return afterwards to their usual steady, day-to-day lawless businesses.

But for a hearty, one-off fee and a hike to their all-round reputation, the job would be properly contracted and done. That is, they'd see off someone for causing irritation or fright or envy to a major, undainty figure, who'd pay cash up front and out of self-interest keep his or her gob shut when the body was found. Ralph gathered that almost always the selected method was gunfire from very close range (clean), though now and then it could be a machete (spurt-prone) or double-hand strangling (laborious). The people who succeeded in this kind of work were flexible and versatile. For instance, a machete was a very large knife and not easy to conceal when approaching the target and trying to look comradely or even affable. This skill had to be learned and practised. Ralph considered the primitive label 'hitman' stupidly unsubtle for such on-tap flair.

Hazel Harpur's visit to The Monty at around two a.m. had seemed to Ralph full of meaning and, in a complicated way, turned his memory towards so-called hitmen. She'd been talking to bouncers at The Monty's main entrance when he first saw her. The street lighting was not bad and he could see that she was fair-haired, broad-faced, slim and athletic-looking, early or mid-teens. She wore a navy jogging suit and scuffed trainers. Of course, he hadn't known at the time who she was. He had thought the bouncers were correct to stop her going into the club. She looked too young and, in any case, The Monty was about to close for the night.

Ralph had considered it wrong that a young girl should be out here now, apparently bickering with Monty sentries. Naturally, this didn't mean he thought there was anything unwholesome about the club, though. The Monty was a prized social asset and would soon push its grand standards higher still. But he'd felt this to be no place for a child so late. He was particularly troubled because the club, despite its established, fine character, had suffered that unsavoury, barbaric, thuggish episode recently. Even before going over to talk to the bouncers and the girl, a so-far unexplainable dread had possessed him in case her arrival had something to do with that disgusting collapse of decorum and order, and also something to do with Assistant Chief Constable (Operations) Desmond Iles.

Ralph had begun to see a kind of depressing message in this string of unpleasant events, as though they signalled the onset of substantial, sickening chaos. Ralph frequently thought he sensed chaos very close. At present this fear had a mysterious, hard grip on him. And so the move of his thoughts towards hitmen he had known and could probably call on for a bit of *ad hocery*.

It angered Ralph that someone who'd started that Monty riot might have caused such strange, fretful behaviour from Hazel Harpur. He regarded it as part of the looming chaos that was on its rapid way. He found himself sympathizing with Mansel Shale's updated survey of the crisis. Perhaps he was right and something should be done about such an odious, dangerous slob. Somewhere he had a number for one of the hitmen.

Ember had walked over to where the bouncers and girl were talking. It always saddened Ralph that The Monty was the kind of club needing bouncers. Intermittently, though, it did. A couple of them were present on that night of carnage, but he couldn't say they'd been effective. True, they were outnumbered.

Tonight, the older bouncer, Felix – white, bald, grey mous-tached – waved a hand towards Ralph and said to the girl, 'Here's Mr Ember now. He's the owner. I expect he'll explain why you can't go in.' He turned to Ralph. 'She says she's Hazel Harpur.'

'Harpur?' Ralph said.

'Yes, we all recognize that name, don't we?' Felix said and laughed.

'You know my dad, do you?' Hazel said. 'He's a cop.'

'Yes, he's fairly famous,' the other bouncer, Jerome, replied. Black, shortish, wiry.

'I meet your father now and then,' Ember had said. 'Usually in the way of business.'

'It's because of the club's business that I came,' Hazel had said.

'And does your dad know you're here?' Jerome said.

'Information,' Hazel replied. 'I thought there might be information.'

'What kind of information?' Ralph said.

'General.'

'General?'

'To do with the trouble at your club,' she said. 'That TV programme et cetera.'

Jerome and Felix had reached the end of their shift and moved away.

'The fighting and destruction I heard about,' Hazel said.

'Heard where?' Ralph said.

'The rumour is around,' she said.

'Oh, rumour. I don't think you should listen to that sort of rubbish, Hazel,' Ember replied. Except for the hair shade, he couldn't see any resemblance in Hazel to her father. Harpur was sometimes described as like a fair-haired Rocky Marciano, the undefeated world heavyweight boxing champion. Hazel's nose remained immaculate. Not many boxers could match this. Hazel's was so sweetly shaped that Ralph couldn't think of it as simply something to sniff with and draw in air. Her nostrils were eloquent. Ralph was always ready to worship a lovely female nose.

'It's all about two murders,' she'd said.

Ember wished the bouncers hadn't left. He felt exposed and conspicuous talking alone to this child in this place at this time and about these topics. While Felix and Jerome were present, it would have seemed to anyone watching merely a debate over whether this youngster should be admitted to the club. Now, it had become deeper and dodgier. He'd avoid going deeper still. Ralph did sometimes back off from going deeper into a situation, and this, tonight, probably rated as a situation. He said: 'I'll call a taxi to take you home now, Hazel. Your father will be anxious.'

'He doesn't know I'm at The Monty,' she said.

'You shouldn't be here now, regardless.'

'Oh, *regardless*, oh, *shouldn't*. Who cares about shouldn't?'

Ralph did. 'I'll get one of the women staff to go with you.'

Later, as he drove home to Low Pastures after locking up the club, he recalled the kind of problems he'd had with one of his own daughters of about Hazel Harpur's age. He reckoned that most of these troubles were romantic/sexual. Perhaps that's what was behind events tonight. Hazel Harpur had said she wanted information, and when he'd asked about what, she'd clammed up. 'General' she'd said – general and to do with The Monty roughhouse not long ago. How to do with it? No detail came. 'General' told him nothing, and was meant to tell him nothing.

There'd been a mention of the television show. Did she mean information about that – information on viewers' reactions to it? In a crafty, devious way, the programme featured Iles, didn't it, Iles disguised but very recognizable? Was the information she wanted centred on him, and centred on what people thought of him? Good God, a link between Iles and Hazel Harpur? The notion rocked him. Confusion still savaged his mind, but not quite so much now. Did Iles have a thing about girls' noses, too?

TWENTY-FOUR

Iles called at Harpur's home next morning while he, Denise and his daughters were just finishing breakfast in the kitchen. Iles had a very, very brief way of ringing the door bell, as though a joyous and massive welcome was guaranteed and so formalities were hardly needed.

Hazel looked sleep-deprived, but Harpur and Denise had decided not to mention what went on in the night. If Hazel wanted to talk about it, she would. She was entitled to some privacy. Although Harpur spent half his life trying to dig out other people's secrets, he didn't include his children's. Anyway, Harpur knew he and Denise were only part of the story. By the time they reached The Monty after Denise rang, it was shut down, the name-plate unlit and measly looking. They saw nobody.

The girls loved it when Denise stayed overnight and cooked eggs, bacon and beans. Her stopovers were only intermittent: quite often she returned to her room at Jonson Court. Hazel and Jill felt breakfast with her and Harpur at Arthur Street was like family. Harpur thought this might not delight Denise, that she wouldn't want a role as mother-figure to kids not much younger than herself. But she never objected.

Today, Iles was in civvy clothes – a navy, wide-lapelled blazer and lightweight beige trousers, check shirt, silver striped blue tie, no scarf, glinting brown lace-up shoes. He reminded Harpur of a door-to-door salesman who'd persuaded his mother to buy on instalments the eight volumes of Arthur Mee's *Children's Encyclopedia*, to his father's fury.

One of the notable things about the ACC was that he had a great range of voice tones, running effortlessly from boundless, blaring contempt for the person he was in conversation with, to sweetly smooth, bull-shitting chumminess. He said now in a cuddly register he used sometimes to lull people, 'Saw you doing a bit of a scour around Idylls during the night,

Col. I didn't want to interrupt at the time, but I do wonder what it was about. Seemed purposeful. Well, how could it be other than purposeful? My impression was you were urgently looking for something or somebody. The urgency goes without saying, really – a search at that hour, and at the property of a very senior Operations officer. In case there had been some sort of incident, I rang the Control Room, but no. A puzzle. I reasoned it must be personal, and best dealt with here. I'm always looking for an excuse to visit, aren't I?'

'Around Idylls?' Hazel said. It sounded as though she had expected something startling from Iles, but not quite this. She'd looked shocked when he arrived and more shocked now.

'I should think he was looking for Haze,' Jill said.

'Shut it, louse,' Hazel said.

'I felt pretty certain it was you, Col,' Iles said. 'That haircut and the yokel style of walk . . . Was Hazel missing?' Iles said. Harpur brought him a chair from another room.

'She came back in a car, maybe a taxi,' Jill said. 'I pretended to be blotto.' Harpur knew he should have guessed Jill might not choose silence, even if he and Denise did. She believed in disclosure and sharp blab.

'Came back in a taxi from where?' Iles said.

'You could ask *her*,' Jill replied. 'And then another car – Dad's I expect,' Jill replied. 'Lights on in the house. I could see the gleam under my bedroom door.'

'How long were they away, Denise and your dad?' Iles said.

'Idylls would be one of the first places he'd think of if Haze had disappeared,' Jill replied.

'Why?' Iles said.

'Oh, you know,' Jill said.

'Do I?' Iles said.

'Don't play dumb. You're not,' Jill said. 'Dad would be very worried. But I can tell Haze is very worried, too, although she wouldn't say. She's a bit like that.'

'Worried about what?' Iles said.

'You, most likely,' Jill said. 'She's loyal.'

'I?' Iles replied.

Hazel rattled a spoon in her cup. The others turned towards her. 'Listen,' she said, 'we're all messing about here, aren't we?'

'Are we?' Iles said.

'I get a feeling,' Hazel said. Harpur saw she might like secrecy, but not if she sensed that others might know more than she did.

'Feeling?' Jill said.

'This is a feeling that Dad and maybe Denise know where I went in the night,' Hazel said.

'Idylls,' Jill replied.

'That's what they seem to have thought first of all,' Hazel said, 'but afterwards.'

'There was an afterwards?' Iles asked.

'Yes. I came home from it in the taxi with an escort, didn't I?'

'Well, Jill thought a taxi,' Iles said.

'And on the way, the escort gets a message on her mobile to say there'd been someone asking if a missing girl had turned up there. Me. Or I, as you'd say.'

'A taxi from where?' Iles said.

'The Monty club,' Hazel said. 'I think it was Denise and Dad asking about the girl, but by the time they got to the club we'd all left. I was in the taxi, paid for by Mr Ember.'

'Yes, Denise guessed that's where you'd be,' Harpur said.

'But why The Monty?' Iles said.

'She worries about you,' Jill said. 'She still thinks about you often, and she's scared you might get done for those terrible crimes, like in the TV play. Some people think you should be. She was looking for anyone who might know stuff about all that, weren't you, Haze? There's a lot of talk in school. Arguments. Nastiness. Accusations. Haze wants the truth, as long as it's the right truth, *her* truth, saying no you didn't do it. Tricky.'

Denise had to get away to a university lecture and Hazel and Jill to school. Hazel said nothing more. Harpur would wash up. He poured Iles a cup of tea.

'That's a real compliment, Col,' Iles said.

'What is, sir?'

'Your daughter was missing, so you thought of me.'

'I didn't know *what* to think.'

'But Denise – very acute. I can see you'd need someone

like that. And true greatness from Ralph, wasn't there, Col? A saint. However, didn't we always know that among drugs tycoons he's unique? The taxi, the chaperone. Oh, well done, well done, Ralphy! This is also the same Ralph W. Ember who has weighty letters in the local press about river pollution and the environment.'

'Yes, kind,' Harpur said.

'Plus some shame.'

'Shame?'

'Shame because the violence at his revered club the other night should have so upset a young girl like Hazel that she had to see the site of it, perhaps find people who could tell her first-hand about it. Denise spotted this link, didn't she?'

'And then there's the other link, isn't there, sir?' Harpur replied.

'Which, Col?'

'The link to you. The ructions started because someone said you'd got away with murder – murders.'

'Yes, I gather someone did,' Iles said.

'Hazel wouldn't like to hear such things about you,' Harpur said.

'I don't like them either,' Iles replied.

'I don't suppose so,' Harpur said.

'That sod hurting Hazel, poor kid. I can't have this.'

'How it is, though,' Harpur replied.

'A lovely kid given bad pain. No, I can't have this, Col.'

TWENTY-FIVE

Inscribed plaques lined a wall at headquarters that led into a reception area commemorating officers killed on duty. The plaques gave simply the name and date his or her life was ended. A non-religious service of remembrance open to the families and friends of each officer was held on the death anniversary. These little ceremonies had breezily become known as halo parades.

There was naturally a plaque for the undercover detective Raymond Cordovan Street, murdered while on an assignment for Iles and Harpur, though mainly for Iles. An assistant chief wouldn't normally get so close to the details of an operation, even though he was Operations, but the risks in this kind of work had always gravely fretted Iles and he gave every under-cover project his full focus, ready to withdraw the spy at any sign of discovery. Just the same, he wasn't always quick enough. Obviously. This he didn't forgive himself for.

Amy Rouse Zole, a middling-to-upper-middling Home Office staffer, came down this year from London with a couple of well-groomed dogsbodies, specifically to talk to Iles about the Raymond Cordovan Street plaque. It must have been decided that this was too sensitive a subject to be dealt with by phone or email. Although Harpur attended the meetings, they were directed mainly and, as if respect-fully, at the ACC.

Amy Rouse Zole said: 'I'd like, if I may, to declare from the outset that these conversations are no more than that, advisory conversations, informal though meaningful confabs. I'm here to moot a point of view, the minister's point of view. And this is all it is, a point of view. Our visit – my colleagues' and mine – is meant in a wholly positive spirit to invite other points of view and to juxtapose these, align these, against the minister's and see how the various opinions compare and, possibly, contrast with one another. The minister's contribution is, of course, significant but, to borrow a phrase from a different context, it is what we might call *primus inter pares* – first among equals.'

Harpur, watching Iles during this creepy, bogus diffident, throat-clearing lyric, saw no ferocity and/or disgust in his face, but he would almost certainly be experiencing one or both. That word '*primus*' – first – when used to describe the status and mouthings of someone other than himself was sure to tear cruelly into his soul, and the fact that this *primus* was only a *primus* among equals would not soothe or fool him. '*Primus* is fucking *primus*, Col, no messing,' Iles would most likely say at now-hear-this volume. He'd suspect that this woman and her high-fly minions had calculatedly taken the long train journey from Whitehall to inflict on him outright personalized degrading – degrading on behalf of a government minister who declined to come and flaunt his fucking *primus*ness himself.

Iles could jemmy his features into non-expression occasionally, but this rarely lasted very long, and was sometimes only a ploy, a manoeuvre. Perhaps Street was such a raw topic for him that it briefly softened his usual authentic barbarism. There were surprising aspects to the ACC's character, and Harpur thought this temporary drift into flagrant self-control might be one of them.

'The minister wonders, Desmond, whether it might be wise and tactful not to run the service for Raymond Cordovan Street,' Amy said. She didn't pause after this, perhaps to prevent Iles answering at once. 'The minister wants me to put the idea to you and to emphasize that it would be a strictly one-off suspension arising from this year's unique circumstances, and limited to the immediate present. "Amy," he said, "be sure, be absolutely sure, to make this point." Of course, he is aware that the proposal could strike some as a slight to the memory of a very gifted and gallant member of your team. But he feels that today's pressures cannot be ignored or gainsaid, and these must condition our thinking and policy now, without creating a precedent.'

'Street's family,' Iles replied.

'The minister certainly has in mind the family,' Amy Zole replied.

'They'll think he's forgotten,' Iles said. 'Reduced to an admittedly tasteful masonry tile. It would be a halo parade without one of the haloes, as though it had time-expired.'

'This is why the minister says for one year only – stresses it's for one year only, a standalone, a blip.'

'Street was wiped out by crooks and now his family will think he's been wiped out by us as well, a grotesque reciprocity,' Iles said. He spoke wearily, as though amazed that Amy and the minister – via Amy – needed to be told any of this.

'That would be entirely wrong – utterly wrong,' Amy Zole said.

'Street has become a liability, so ditch him – that's how it will appear to them. And how it will appear to others. It's how it appears to me, and probably to Col, here, as though the memory of Ray has become a nuisance, and his work valueless. It reminds me of the way politicians busy themselves apologizing for things that happened years ago and in which they were gloriously uninvolved so they can say "sorry" without its meaning anything.'

'The minister recognizes that matters of extreme delicacy are involved,' Amy said. 'He has been in touch by phone with your chief constable, who said the decision for or against a ceremony this year was very much a matter for you.'

'Some call him the Artful Dodger,' Iles said. 'He has the Queen's Police Medal, you know. There was a ceremony when he was presented with it. He didn't seem to object.'

'Perhaps he means well,' Amy said.

Harpur thought she'd be about fifty, with traces of a North of England accent, possibly Tyneside, but overlaid by educated cockney and maybe Oxbridge. She had naturally auburn hair, greying at the edges over her ears, fresh-looking unpitted skin and charmingly presented teeth.

She had on a pale blue linen jacket over a darker blue silk blouse and navy trousers. Her hands were long-fingered with prominent, gleaming knuckles. She wore no rings but a double gold bracelet on her right wrist. Her replies to Iles were given quickly and tidily, as if already packaged, and brought on call from a handy store cupboard. Harpur didn't find this surprising. It would have been easy to forecast how things were likely to go, especially if she had known in advance much about Iles. Home Office chiefs probably *did* know plenty about Iles and, if they had to negotiate with him, got themselves into a state of patience, alertness, and resilience. It would, in fact, be a massive failure of duty if they did *not* know a good deal about Iles.

But Harpur had a feeling that, although her responses to Iles were so neatly assembled, they were also lifeless, inert, reach-me-down. She had a mission to carry out and would do this efficiently, but perhaps didn't believe what she was saying. Civil servants, weren't they always like that? They got briefed by someone with the power to brief and then they passed on that briefing to someone *they* had the power to brief. If Amy didn't swallow what the minister had said, it could explain why those introductory words sounded so clumsy, deadbeat and phony.

The five of them were sitting at one end of the big conference table in Iles's suite at headquarters. Each had a couple of small bottles of spring water and a glass in front of them. Harpur wondered whether the two sidekicks with Amy – Olivia and Vince – were present on the minister's orders, to make sure Amy said and did what she was supposed to say and do. They spoke rarely. They observed, they monitored. At some points in Amy's comments they smiled – smiled together, like from a shared agenda. There was so much double-strength empathy floating about that Harpur felt it could curl his hair.

Amy said: 'In fact, the minister feels that the family might be glad to have the commemoration dropped this year.'

'Has he asked them?' Iles said.

'Would it resurrect old griefs?' Amy replied.

'Did they ever die?' Iles said.

'Controversies reignited,' Amy said.

'Which?' Iles said.

'People ask – the family probably asks – why has nobody been punished for Street's death?' Amy said. 'There's been a television programme.'

'Well, with or without a telly programme, people know that following Street's murder, two villains are dead.' This reply from Iles, if it was one, seemed to stun Amy. It stunned Harpur, also. Iles said: 'But, of course, as Col would no doubt tell us, we should beware of the denounced fallacy, "*Post hoc ergo propter hoc.*"'

'Definitely,' Harpur replied.

'I expect he's dying to translate the Latin for us, but I'll do that instead: "Because something comes later than something else, the second something must have been caused by the first." Clearly, a fallacy, a ridiculous piece of supposed logic. It's absurd, isn't it, to apply this gibberish to the case of the two criminal deados?'

Amy was silent for half a minute. Although she might have been given an outline by her Home Office superiors of what Iles was like, nobody could offer a full understanding of him, or even half an understanding. He prized evasiveness. His. Only his. Amy poured herself some water and took a sip. Then she said: 'Two men are dead, but they are two men who were found not guilty of killing Raymond Cordovan Street.'

'They were, they were,' Iles said.

'But?' Amy said.

'Oh, yes they were found not guilty,' Iles replied.

'That's what I mean by controversy,' she said. 'It's what the minister also regards as controversy.' Olivia and Vince nodded three times each. 'We've seen something of that, haven't we?'

'Something of what?' Iles said.

'Controversy. And more than controversy. Violence at a city club. The Monty, is it called, proprietor Ralph Wyverne Ember? Provocation from the TV film led to unfortunate uproar and damage.'

'Ah, you've had intimations,' Iles said.

'Constituency members of Parliament talk to the minister, as you'd expect. He sees clippings from the local press. The proprietor of the club was deeply offended that it should be the site for such lawlessness. I'm told he is a notable local environmentalist, ardent in the fight against river pollution, and with considerable ambitions for his club – these to an almost idolatrous level. We have to look after such people.'

'I try,' Iles said. 'Anyway, he soon had The Monty back in shape.'

'The minister doesn't want circumstances that could cause

a repeat of such trouble and he believes a service for Street at this time might . . .' She had another pause and another sip, and then with a matey grin at Iles, she said: 'Matters are made additionally volatile because of, if I may say so, Desmond, your own involvement.'

'Yes, you may say. During your researches you've probably noticed that I'm the assistant chief constable (Operations).' But it was pronounced as customary from Iles, assssissstant chief conssstable (Operationsss). 'Three men have been done to death on my ground. How could I not be involved?'

This seemed to Harpur quite a question, but Amy didn't try to answer it, and she got no help from Olivia or Vince.

TWENTY-SIX

Psychology: this was another of Ralph's special interests, alongside cleaner rivers. It involved a delicate but thorough tour of the human mind and not *what* we thought but *how* we thought it. Psychology was one of the subjects in a mature student degree course he'd started at the university, an easy walk from The Monty. He'd completed a Foundation Year but had lately been forced to drop out of classes for a while because of very demanding professional and business pressures; particularly the surge in sales of Impressive Bessy, affectionate slang name for a bonny brand of coke. He found, though, that he could still apply some of that early teaching to his own life.

Shock – and the way the brain and psyche dealt with it – was a topic that intrigued him, for example his reaction to that gross behaviour the other night at the club; or, more, accurately, reactions, plural. They came in two stages. This matched exactly what a college lecture described as 'standard pattern' when someone tried to cope with shock. First, at The Monty there had been the rush to counter, nullify, cancel, conceal the sickening results of the violence by emergency repairs and replacements so the club could quickly restore normal service for members. It was what the lecturer, quoting some American poet, had called 'the lust for order' – compulsive, instinctive, automatic.

The second response came subsequently and went very much deeper, convincing Ember, naturally, that he must immediately get in touch with one of the hitmen he remembered from his knockabout days in London at the beginning of his career. Surely Naunton (Waistcoat) Favard could not be allowed to continue or, putting it another, more straightforward way, allowed to stay alive, blurting his damn grievances. OK, they were genuine grievances, but did he imagine everyone wanted to hear about them, for God's sake? Hadn't he heard

of stiff upper lips? His lips couldn't be stiff because they had
to frame around and produce those damn screeches of indig-
nation and resentment. This was egomania. This was incivility.
Ralph loathed incivility.

His thoughts came in two sections, binary as they would
be termed in lectures:

(a) Favard must be got rid of because he wanted Iles
charged, tried and jailed for what Favard believed to be the
killing of his brother, Paul, and Cliff Jamieson. He would
do everything he could to fix it. Ralph sympathized a bit.
Brotherly love was traditionally noble and very powerful.
But it could also be a pest. If Waistcoat succeeded and Iles
was removed, how could business continue to prosper so
sweetly? The trade, the vocation, needed him, and in return
the trade made sure the city's parks, discos, streets, housing
estates, public libraries, arcades, squares, religious rallies,
back lanes stayed peaceful and reasonably safe. This was
the simple, elegant, balancing arrangement that everyone in
the commercial scene understood and cherished. It must not
be endangered. Iles kept the city from falling into chaos.
Waistcoat ought to realize this. He did not have the right to
act in restraint of trade by getting Iles taken away. Ralph
thought of Mansel Shale and the fury and fear he displayed
at any possibility of losing the assistant chief constable
(Operations) and his fine constructive outlook.

(b) But as with psychology there was another, more profound
aspect. What enraged Ralph was the insult, even contempt,
that Naunton Favard had revealed towards The Monty by
choosing the club as location for that totally hate-based, vandal-
izing, anti-Iles demonstration. Waistcoat would regard The
Monty as merely a building – a suitable venue for his
venomous, bite-back pageant. He probably knew nothing about
Ralph's unwavering plans for the glorious transformation of
the club into a place of quiet distinction, rating with The
Athenaeum or The Reform or any other elite club in London
or New York. Even if Waistcoat did appreciate some of this,
he would probably still have pushed on with his foul, anarchic
scheme to stir up lay-waste Hunnishness at The Monty, regardless of the club's honour and prestige. He would not grasp that

Ralph's Monty was not so much a social facility – though that was an important, wholesome role – but an idea, a concept, a symbol. Ralph had an inescapable duty to protect it. To ignore this responsibility would be flagrant dereliction. As well as building a new personality for The Monty, he was building a new personality for himself, and there was something almost holy about that.

He came to think, in that second-stage result of a shock, that Naunton Favard's actions the other night amounted to a kind of blasphemy. If churches had pool tables in the nave, would any of the congregation consider it a tolerable jape to tip the table over, seriously injuring a woman who – through no fault of her own – happened to be in the wrong spot when it fell? True, the table had been righted quickly enough in the first-stage reaction, but the effect on Ralph persisted and now cried out for a different, more fundamental response. Ralph saw blatant foolishness in Naunton Favard's campaign. Three people had already been killed. Perhaps these deaths invited another, as deaths in the trade often did.

Although Ralph owned a couple of Walther automatics and had been given a choice of other pistols by Mansel, he'd decided it would be better to get someone else to see off Waistcoat. Ralph hadn't fired a gun for a long time. He thought that possibly he'd still be accurate with a weapon across a short distance, but it might not be like this with Waistcoat. In any case, this wasn't the kind of role Ralph regarded as suitable for himself now. He was a considerable businessman and famed environmentalist – several rivers were cleaner because of him. He would not be surprised if he were offered in due course a knighthood. He would not be so foolishly big-headed as to expect this distinction immediately, but he thought he could move steadily towards it by, for instance, receiving an Order of the British Empire. Environment was definitely a goer. He loved the word 'limpid', as applied to rivers he'd had some part in freshening up.

He ran a fine club which, as a matter of fact, was the main cause of his anger towards Naunton Favard. Ember believed that when you reached a certain level in life you deputed, you didn't scramble about managing details. That would be a pathetic waste of your core strength. You observed, you put your brain to work, not your body, and said what was needed, then passed the actual labour to an expert, a specialist. It was one of the privileges of success. Kings no longer rode into battle at the head of their troops.

There could also be an age factor, though Ralph didn't want to think about that too much. He might have handled the whole project, including the actual Waistcoat death, if he still had a young man's energy and daring. He recognized that some of these had dwindled. There'd be no joy any longer from seeing someone he'd shot tumble to the ground, even though he'd like to hear that someone else had brought about this happy result on one of Ralph's enemies (e.g. above all, Waistcoat).

When looking for a hitman, Ralph had to realize that, as in his own case, people he'd known and worked with in the London days might have had big changes to their lives since. During that time Ralph had moved the family out of London; established a very robust recreational substances business; started a university degree; bought Low Pastures, his manor house, cash down; and, above all, acquired and developed a prestige club, The Monty, and was soon to increase that prestige exponentially. The London colleagues and friends would probably also have had big advances in their careers, or failed and disappeared – were maybe locked up somewhere. Ralph had known hitmen might be difficult to find, or could be impossible to find. Their addresses and phone numbers would not be in the directories.

A few regulars at The Monty had businesses that took them to London occasionally and Ralph asked if they could point him towards a couple of contacts there just to 'give me something of an overview' and 'reintroduce me to the general scene.' This was the kind of cloudy, evasive language used by almost everyone in The Monty when talking about matters that needed to be cloudy and evasive, and there were plenty of matters that needed to be cloudy and evasive. He got two names. They wouldn't be angels: Lance Staple, Frank Quade-Hont. Ralph thought he should be able to start some useful parley with them and do a little sentimentalizing about Ralph's past. He could wait during these chats until mentions of people he'd known came up – and known for the sort of reasons that might help him now. Ralph thought it would take at least a week to find someone available, qualified and willing. And affordable? That wouldn't bring problems. Ralph believed in spending on good causes and this one was better than good: exemplary. It was the future. It was preservation of what had already been achieved despite resistance and obstruction, and which must not be lost by carelessness.

There might be some difficulties with Margaret, his wife. The thought of Ralph on his own in London for a week – flashing his Charlton Heston features and his money – might make her uneasy. But Margaret had known for a long while that there were aspects of Ralph's business it was best she stayed ignorant of. He thought Margaret probably reproached herself for this – regarded it, perhaps, as cowardice. But he didn't see how the marriage could work otherwise, and Margaret most likely agreed. She didn't press any inquiries about the London trip. He'd definitely bring her back something worthwhile from Bond Street. They had terrific arcades in that district, with brilliant stuff behind shatterproof window glass.

But he mustn't overdo the expense or she'd think he had a lot to compensate for. He half wished he could be honest with her. That would mean involvement in a possible killing, though, and he felt he mustn't do that. The marriage service asked for loyalty in sickness and in health, not complicity in a slaughter.

Although he wanted one, Ralph considered the term 'hitman' unpleasant. It described accurately enough what they did – hitmen hit – but he thought the label could be more tactful, less graphic. On the other hand, some vocab in the murder area was absolutely OK by Ralph. Take 'contract'. Ember didn't in the least mind the phrase saying a contract was out on somebody, and he dearly hoped to place one on Naunton Fazard. It meant a killer had been hired for a fee to see that somebody off, usually by shooting, but hits could also be by knife, machete, axe or strangulation. Ralph felt the word 'contract' made an assignment sound like any properly drawn-up commercial deal. It was as if this particular deal commissioned a killer to carry out the task and named the money terms: a non-returnable, 50 per cent down payment, the rest on completion, no stamp duty.

And, of course, Ralph's decision to engage a paid help *was* a commercial move, its objective clear and precise, to safeguard the firms of himself and Mansel Shale by seeing to it that Naunton Favard was permanently stopped from making terrible allegations in public about the assistant chief.

It all went reasonably well in London and, after a couple of evenings drinking with his new colleagues, he heard a name he did know from the past, Milan Parvin. 'Ah, yes, Mil, what's he up to these days?' Ralph said, with a warm ex-chummy smile.

'Wallpaper and paint, or that's the bit he shows. A shop out Kingsbury way,' Frank said. 'Jo's And Mil's – Jo's his partner.'

'Is he still . . . well . . . busy?' Ralph replied.

'There's a lot of refurbishing of London properties,' Lance Staple replied. 'Houses getting spruced up for sale. Big money. There's non-stop demand for decorators' stuff.'

'No, I meant . . . *busy*,' Ralph said.

'We know what you meant,' Frank said.

'Oh, yes, of course we do,' Lance said.

They didn't add to that.

As Ralph recalled, there was an Italian branch of Mil's family and he'd been christened Milan, apparently, but not many used the full geography except, maybe, his mother. Ralph thought of Parvin as a lad, and that's what he had been the last time Ralph had any dealing with him. Now, he would be late-twenties, possibly into good money from somewhere undeclared, and owner of the décor firm, for cover. After all, that's what wallpaper and paint did – cover.

During Ralph's early spell working in London there'd been whispers around following what had seemed to be a couple of execution-type killings linked to some gang turmoil. Mil's name had come up. Several of the whispers spoke of him, spoke admiringly. One of the judgments Ralph remembered was, 'So young, yet work so very neat.' Ralph hoped this meant he'd be even neater now.

'Mil's pricey these days,' Lance Staple said.

'For the paint and paper?' Ralph said.

'Sort of,' Frank said.

'It's more to do with the personal service side of things,' Lance said. 'He can give rare, high skill. Plus, of course, he's using his own equipment. Insists. Has to have familiarity. It costs. Most customers are willing to pay the extra for reliability. Everything's built in to the global invoice – an invoice in his head. Nothing's written down, obviously. Cash preferred. He'll take fifties. Many won't – fear of imitations. He says it's a risk business, and that's one of the risks. Get yourself a game-keeper's jacket, Ralph – pockets big enough to take man-traps or a lot of sterling.'

Psychology, psychology – Ralph sometimes tried to figure what the personality of a hitman must be like. Of course, there would be very long periods of his life when the hitman wasn't a hitman at all. This was especially true of the hitman type Ralph had met: they did a job and then went back to another job, their main one. They seemed able to switch on the ability and the resolve for this one commission, and then put them away until next time. They had no motivation other than money. The hitman in a film called *The Day of the Jackal*, which Ralph had watched on one of the movie channels, only got busy in the plot to kill de Gaulle when he knew the up-front fee had been paid into his Swiss bank account. He had no politics, no enmity towards de Gaulle. He was a target only, replacing a grapefruit the hitman used for a practice shot and which exploded into bits when the bullet hit it.

There were different kinds of execution. The kind Ralph wanted for Naunton Favard couldn't be compared with what an official hangman used to do. He acted on behalf of the state against someone who had been tried and convicted. The hangman was a sort of civil servant. But the hitman was a private hireling who killed somebody he might know nothing about, and who'd not been found guilty by any jury. It surely required an unusual mind to adapt so easily and efficiently.

'Why, Ralphy!' Mil yelled as Ember walked into the shop. Mil was standing near a pyramid of multi-size water-based indoor-use paint pots. 'Your choice is our command,' said a board at the heap's summit. A woman, about twenty-five, fair-haired, slight, small-featured, pretty, was alongside him.

'Ralphy?' she said. 'Should I know him?'

'Ralphy Ember,' Parvin replied. 'Ralph, this is Jo, my, as it were, manager.'

The egomaniac, snappy way she had put that question really angered Ralph. 'Should I know him?' It was as though she considered Ralph didn't exist unless she had looked him over, found him reasonably OK, and filed him away for a future occasion such as now, but had forgotten about it because Ralph was so insignificant. That wasn't the kind of reception he normally expected from women of all ages. He was used to them reacting with startled, gusset-damping delight at first meeting Ralph because of his indisputable resemblance to Charlton Heston, occasionally in films on TV. There would often be a sort of follow-up to that: many would show an intense curiosity about that long scar on one side of his face. Ralph never spoke about it, never disclosed how he had received it. He thought they must wonder and speculate and imagine. That old wound gave him mystery, and seemingly many women wanted to crack that mystery. Ralph didn't mind. Women were entitled to be fascinated by him.

Jo abruptly moved away from Mil and walked fast through an avenue of varnish cans towards Ember. He felt confused. Perhaps he had been wrong to think of her as a self-obsessed and arrogant bitch after all. Was she coming as so many had in the past to cosset his wound-trace and generally make up to him, although Mil was there – and was almost certainly more than a shop colleague?

Ralph resolved to be kindly to her. He understood why he had this effect on numerous women. It definitely wasn't something he sought or worked at. He'd regard that as crude and tiresome. On the Foundation Year course at uni he had come across the Latin phrase, *sui generis*, meaning one, and only one, of its kind. Didn't that describe him well? If his home didn't already have a name, a historic name, Low Pastures, he might have called it *Sui Generis*. He was Ralph Wyverne Ember. That was enough, wasn't it?

But, no, it wasn't. Jo stepped past Ralph and went out into the sort of porch at the shop front. She stopped a few inches short of the pavement. Guardedly, she leaned forward just far

enough to let her scrutinize the street carefully left and right
without getting caught by CCTV. Ralph realized she was
checking to see if he'd been followed. It was another sign that
she didn't care much about him personally, scar or not. She'd
be interested, though, in any tails he'd unconsciously brought.
This slighting attitude Ralph found almost unbelievable.
He wanted to yell that he hadn't come to a rubbishy bit of
London from his unmortgaged manor house, Low Pastures,
once lived in by a Spanish consul, for some strutting little
piece to insult him. She obviously didn't think Ralph was
sharp enough to know whether he had led someone here, or
more than one. She regarded him as a liability, not an *El Cid*
figure, as played by Heston.

She came back into the shop. 'I look after the other side of
Milan's business,' she said.

'Which other side?' Ralph said.

'Not the paint,' she said.

'The paper?' Ralph said.

'Not the paper, either,' Jo said.

'You know how it is, Ralph,' Mil said.

'How what is?' Ralph replied.

'Jo approaches things in a very positive way,' Mil said.

'Which things?' Ralph said.

'You wouldn't be in these parts, and in this shop, if it wasn't
for something a bit out of the ordinary,' Mil said.

'That's why I come into it,' Jo said.

'Into what?' Ralph said.

'You're here for something special,' Jo replied. 'Great! We
can handle it, can't we, Mil?'

'We ought to go into the pav,' Mil said.

TWENTY-SEVEN

Ralph had two words in his head. He liked to focus on issues in this way and reduce them to their manageable basics. This was how he got clarity. This was how he decided on priorities, crucial when he had so many interests and projects, such as cleansed rivers; the protection of Assistant Chief Constable (Operations) Desmond Iles; the urgent need of a hitman; his children's schooling, with special emphasis on the golden apples and other classical tales.

One of the words preoccupying him now was 'pav', as used by Mil, and 'unmortgaged', the other. Well, pav wasn't really a word, but a fraction of a word. Although Ralph felt baffled by it for a few moments, he discovered it meant 'pavilion', and referred to a kind of brick-built, tiled-roof outhouse in the back yard of Mil's shop. The interior was luxurious – well-padded garden chairs, a china and glassware cabinet, a miniature bar, and a deep-pile dark blue carpet.

'Away from the hustle and bustle of the shop,' Mil said. 'Staff can get on with that.'

A rectangle of three-ply timber, painted to look like a section of rendered wall, stood on an easel near the bar. 'We have a stack of these boards to help customers choose a colour for the outside of their property,' Jo said. 'They can relax while making up their minds. They should be able to say to themselves, "This is a tint I can live with, and not just live *with* but live *in*, because these treated walls will close around me as occupant. Therefore this tint must harmonize not just with the property but with myself."'

So fucking what? That's how Ralph would have liked to reply. OK, he recognized that these two needed a respectable, semi-genuine business to help account for their loot, but he could do without the flowery, lunatic details. He would have liked to mention that Low Pastures, his beautiful, time-graced home, residence of so many folk of distinction through

the ages, was mostly authentic old stone as well as unmortgaged – that other word – and didn't require tarting up with
any of their damn here-today-and-gone-the-year-after-next
gaudy shades, thank you very much. 'Interesting,' was all he
actually said, though. These were complicated people. He had
to take things slowly and gently with them. He could remember
Mil and his name from that previous time, but he had no
dossier on him. He did dossiers on people now, but that was
part of running a large business – part of a career that had so
considerably expanded since those fledgling days.

'And the pav can give us privacy for other kinds of business,'
Jo said, 'meaning yours, Ralph. We are, as it were, the children
of the pav as, say, some tribes might call themselves children of
the tundra or of the rain forest.'

Mil brought a bottle of Krug from a fridge behind the bar.
To Ralph, the popping cork seemed to signal the start of a
party, innocent and cheery, or alternatively was like a single,
killing shot from a silenced pistol. Jo took three flutes
out of the cabinet. Mil poured. Jo lifted her glass and said:
'Here's to happy cooperation and an untroubled outcome.'
They drank, standing respectfully for the toast, and then sat
down in the lounge chairs.

'Forgive me if I spell out the obvious, but you want
someone dead, Ralphy, right?' Mil said. 'I can see it in your
face. I've come to recognize the signs after so long in this
bold occupation. Around the eyes I see a mix of regret that
the wipe-out should be necessary, and a certainty that it *is*
necessary, this certainty coming over quite a bit stronger
than the regret or there'd be impasse. Well, if the regret
signs were stronger, you wouldn't be here anyway, since
you'd have no proper commitment to the annihilation. As
we've said, Ralphy, why else would you have made the trip
to London and our premises? I expect we're in your filing
system under "Removal Firms".'

Ralph hated to be called Ralphy. He believed it made him
sound like somebody's half-witted cousin. He thought he
might have winced when Mil introduced him as Ralphy.
Perhaps Jo had noticed. When she spoke next it was with a
good, beefy emphasis on his y-free name. This woman had

a brain and sensitivity. 'Ralph, we wouldn't have bothered bringing you out to the pav if Mil didn't judge you someone worth helping and ready to meet our substantial but reasonable overhead costs.'

'Thanks,' Ember said.

'More than one?' Jo asked.

'Just the one,' Ralph said. 'Why do you expect a number?'

'We get all sorts here,' Jo said. 'Plurals are not rare. They're difficult, of course they are, especially if they have to be done simultaneously, on the same day and in the same location, which is sometimes the case. Our client might want to destroy a whole family or the executive board of a substantial gang. We get this kind of request – multiples – when people want to use the togetherness of the deaths to make a special, scary sense. It will appear to be saying there are plenty more wipe-outs like this one if, say, a certain behaviour isn't improved – usually, of course, behaviour to do with money or women, sometimes money and women. We need forewarning, not just so we can cater for ammunition quantity, but the geography and landscape when it's multiples may be quite different from a simple solitary pop. Because the setting is likely to be more extensive, we have to expect the possible and potentially awkward presence of other people not at all involved in the hit but a possible nuisance. It's why I always bring in a numerical query early on. We like to visualize surroundings – a setting – with as much detail as possible.'

'Baden-Powell provided the logo for hitmen and hitwomen. "Be prepared, especially if you're doing more than one",' Mil said.

'Have we got a name for this one-off?' Jo asked.

'Favard. Naunton Favard.' Ralph said.

'We don't need to know why you'd like him taken out,' Jo said, 'but we'll be Googling the name, as you'd expect, so if there are special factors it might be useful if we're made aware of them today. Now, Ralph, you're obviously going to ask, what type of special factors? This is a completely reasonable response. Minders, for instance – does the target have close protection? Is it twenty-four hours? Is it more than one and, if so, how many? Do we know whether the target goes armed? If so, what with and where is it carried, at the waist, shoulder holster, in a sock?'

'I can't answer many of those queries,' Ralph said. 'But I can give you the one important basic: his brother was murdered. That's Paul Favard.'

Mil was already Googling on his phone. 'Paul Favard. Clifford Jamieson, both killed. I don't have anything to say the case was solved.'

'No,' Ralph said.

'So, Naunton Favard thinks he knows who did his brother and will deal with it because the courts have failed to,' Mil said. 'That it? There's a vengeance element, a strong vengeance element. There often is. People cease to believe in the legal offices and decide to do the job themselves – or, more likely, decide to brief an outfit like ours to do it for them. But I don't see how this example affects you, Ralphy.'

'Naunton Favard has become a nuisance,' Ralph said.

'In what way?' Jo said.

'Business,' Ralph replied.

'But you'd rather not say how?' Jo replied.

So very right. Ralph would rather not say how. To say how would mean bringing Iles into the chat. This Ralph knew he must not do. The whole and absolute reason for his trip here was to keep Iles securely in place, his influence brilliant, reliable and secret.

'The target – easy to find?' Mil asked.

'Probably,' Ralph said. Mansel Shale had 'asked around', as he called it, and mentioned an address for Naunton Favard. Ralph gave it to Jo and Mil now to memorize, no writing down.

'Several further standard questions if you don't mind, Ralph,' Jo said. 'Have you hired, commissioned, asked anyone else to carry out this assignment?'

'No.'

'Have you spoken to anyone about it?'

'No.'

'Do you know of anyone who might, independently of you, be planning to see off Naunton Favard?'

Well, there was Mansel Shale, and Mansel Shale's gun store. And there was Iles who'd been enraged that Waistcoat had brought pain to Hazel Harpur, and who might already have experience of executions. 'No,' he said.

'Vengeance is a very tricky area,' Jo said.

Mil went to an open-topped box near the bar where they kept the colour option boards. He rummaged for a while and then picked one out. He replaced the board already on the easel with it. The new board was entirely different from the previous one. Instead of a wall section, this board displayed a graph made by a series of columns of different heights and in a range of shades. On the left upright was a series of escalating numbers climbing in units of five thousand.

'A quick representation of our charges, Ralph,' Jo said. 'We obviously can't label the columns in case of police curiosity one day, but I can give you an indication of what each stands for, and you can see for yourself how it's priced by reading the figure on the upright. I have to stress that these are prices today. We cannot guarantee to hold them at that level if there are delays and changes in the general economic situation, for instance, possible inflationary pressures.'

As she spoke she pointed to the appropriate parts of the diagram. 'The fees range from the simplest, uncomplicated, single-shot death in a favourable location – the pale green column – to, say, a plural assignment in difficult surround-ings and on the same date – this crimson column. In your case, Ralph, I think it's the mauve here: a solo target, choice of location left to us, no tracing problem, you say, but a vengeance complication. Vengeance can mean there's a lot of malevolence around. It can go on and on, *sine die*, tit-for-tat.'

'Corny pun possible on *die*,' Mil said.

'Where vengeance is the theme, there's likely to be uncon-trolled spreading of retaliation, reciprocity in stage after stage, especially where there are big families concerned,' Jo said. 'We might get some of the peril ourselves if the job isn't managed perfectly. So, we have to add a premium for venge-ance. The short, turquoise column shows the premium. We'd be using our own equipment, of course, so I'd say we are talking about this point here on the upright: a charge of 30K. GB Pounds. We supply and use our own equipment, swear a gagging oath in case of arrest, all *compris*.'

'Well, talk,' Ralph replied.

TWENTY-EIGHT

They did talk, though not for long. Ralph considered it would be disgracefully poor taste to spend time haggling over price. After all, this discussion concerned someone's very life and how to snuff it out. Naunton Favard was toe jam, but, like any human, or near-human, he could be helped along to a more or less dignified death. The extremely respectable fee earmarked for his extinction would help eke such last-ditch dignity on to the former shit-stirring sod. OK, so no question he had a dead brother. But did he think he was the only one who'd suffered that kind of loss? Did he imagine his commonplace grief excused the terrible damage he'd caused to The Monty's prestige interior, including abuse of a pool table leading to rib breakage? This was egomania. Wasn't this perversion? Values? He wouldn't know what the word meant.

As a matter of fact, Ralph thought Mil would demand more than £30,000, and he'd brought £20,000 for the half down-payment. It was settled that Ralph would deliver the completion tranche within forty-eight hours of hearing Naunton Favard was officially dead. If Ralph wanted a progress report he could telephone, giving the name Sidney Engard Junior, and ask Jo or Mil whether the new consignment of William Morris wallpaper had arrived. That is, had Waistcoat been done?

Ralph wasn't totally comfortable with this coding because someone might ring genuinely wanting William Morris paper. Quite a few people went for all that greenery, tendrils and fronds. Once this paper was in place on the walls of a room, it would be like living inside a healthy bush. Some city people liked to hark back centuries to their rural ancestors, without actually becoming rural. OK, it might not be Sidney Engard Junior ringing, but there was room for confusion. After all, it wouldn't actually be Sidney Engard Junior ringing if Ralph made a call. He thought the arrangements were becoming too complicated.

Mil had said: 'Make sure you add "Junior" to your Engard name. It's a Yank touch, not something we use in this country, so no chance of error. Fortunately you've got a youthful voice. Ralph, a.k.a. Daddy Boy's Sid.'

Yes, Ralph would agree about his voice, one facet of a general, all-round youthfulness. He didn't get the gamekeeper's jacket recommended by Lance Staple, though he had followed Lance's suggestion and gone for fifties. These he distributed in wads around his pockets without spoiling the expensive hang of his custom-made suit. He would hate to have bulges while on a delicate business mission.

When unloading, he had to be subtle. He didn't want Mil and Jo to see he had more with him than they'd asked for. Spontaneously, Jo might think up some new, special risk factor so he'd have to cough another hundred fifties. Ralph made a slow, very methodical handover, planting the packages one by one on the bar. God, how naff to have a bar in a jumped-up garden shed, but he needed this kind of solid platform for the instalment ritual.

Of course, Mil and Jo might regard it as strange that he seemed to know in advance exactly how much they would charge. Or perhaps they'd feel impressed to be dealing with someone who had such brilliantly sharp intuition and accurate instincts. Ralph could believe he did give out that kind of considerable aura. This wasn't something he had to work for. Auras were either there or not. In his case they were and he felt grateful. But it seemed to him that the methodical way he laid the money out for Mil and Jo – the plonking deliberateness – showed there was a nitty-gritty, workmanlike side to him as well as that other mysterious, almost-spiritual flair.

They would be aware of a completeness in him. Although they did not know the detail of why Naunton Favard had to be seen off, they'd certainly understand that only someone very stupid would wilfully offend Ralph Ember. No doubt some of this respect was due to the Charlton Heston resemblance. That could produce a kind of awe in people he met, even if it was for a second, third or more time. But, leaving aside this glorious fluke, Ralph felt he had what could only be termed 'a presence', something that others quickly appreciated and which came from the very core of him, needing no assistance from *Ben Hur* or *El Cid*. Ralph felt that when he was in company, regardless of how large the group, everyone there would sense he was near because of this stunning power of 'presence'. Ralph believed that even people in such a group who had not seen him face to face would be conscious of him nearby, so it could not be a matter of resemblance to Chuck Heston, it was his – Ralph's – own influence. He never spoke of this extraordinary radiance. He was afraid it might sound like vanity to mention it.

Mil and Ralph went back into the main shop, and Mil said in a voice for everyone to hear, 'Those tints you've chosen will set each other off admirably in your home, sir. We will deliver Thursday a.m., in plenty of time for redecorating to commence on the Monday.' He and Ralph shook hands in full view. Ralph was conscious of a special gravity: one of the fingers now clasped by his would be the one that pulled a trigger to finish Waistcoat. In Ralph's opinion this created a remarkable bond, dedicated, temporary and half paid for. It went beyond and beyond again the recent phony merchandising chatter.

Jo stayed behind in the pav, probably to count the money. Although that might seem distrustful and mercenary, Ralph did not blame her. He was a stranger to Jo and she knew nothing about his honesty, or its absence. Of course, she would notice the Charlton Heston likeness, but that didn't really have much to do with business finance. She might need more time to build solid rapport with Ralph. But it did not mean Jo had no interest in sex, merely because she seemed so focused on accountancy. Ralph thought that when he brought the next payment, things might grow more relaxed, Waistcoat being dead, and he could try an approach, if he and Jo should be alone at some point. He thought it would be unkind to treat her as though she had no feelings outside her job. Ralph always recognized that there were undoubted obligations for someone with his extraordinary, flagrant appeal to women.

As he walked back to his car, Ralph enjoyed the memory

of Jo's slightly irregular and very white teeth, and neat, unob-
trusive chin. At the same time, though, he tried to work out
if he was being tailed. He didn't turn to see who exactly was
behind him, but twice in shop windows he noticed the reflection of a man in a beige lightweight jacket and jeans, perhaps
thirty-five years old, mid-height, solidly made, dark hair thin-
ning, thin dark beard.

But this was a busy road with plenty of pedestrians, and
some of those were also reflected in the glass walking after
him. Ralph thought the man he singled out, though, appeared
to keep a very constant space between him and Ralph, made
no attempt to overtake when Ralph slowed to use a crossing
and reach the multi-storey car park on the other side of the
road. The summer jacket also crossed, keeping that same
distance from Ralph and staying with him.

Ralph decided to leave the car where it was for now. He
passed the multi-storey, came to a café, went in and ordered
a coffee. The jacket didn't enter after him – had presumably
continued on while Ralph was opening the café door, his back
to the pavement. He took half an hour over the coffee. The
man was not in sight when Ralph emerged. Had his imagin-
ation been working too hard? He collected his car and drove
out of London and home. He reckoned he'd dealt with Mil
and Jo fairly well, though there were bound to be some stresses,
given the kind of topics they were concerned with. Had those
stresses been more acute than he'd realized? Had they pushed
his mind a bit off balance, made him feel vulnerable and – that
disgusting, appalling sneer from the past – panicky?

TWENTY-NINE

Amy Rouse Zole and her pair of Home Office back-ups stayed overnight, and at the start of the morning meeting she said: 'Ember?'

Harpur thought the word came over as undoubtedly a question, not a statement, but offered no vocab either side to help with meaning. Harpur felt like it was like a voice crying out in the wilderness, a voice of someone knowing things were not right – such as being in a wilderness – but not able to say why or how, only to pipe up with a solo word in search of clarity. Where the fuck had context bolted to? So, one question hatched another, and together they produced nothing.

'To do with Ralph?' Harpur asked – making question three, and not much more than dud repetition; pathetic, really, giving her leadership of the moment: *Please, please, please, tell me what you're getting at, Amy.*

'What to do with Ralph?' Iles said urgently. Four. Another plea. The assistant chief abominated evasive language, unless it was his own and required for a trap.

'Olivia's had an interesting email from the Department,' Amy said. 'They like to prove they never sleep. It's about a murmur they've received from the police. Olivia's in charge of info inflow for me, and Vince has done a polished decrypting job. I travel nowhere without them.'

'Always at your distinguished service, Amy,' Vince said.

'Absolutely,' Olivia said, 'a privilege, indeed, the cause of much envy.'

Harpur couldn't work out whether any two of them, or all three, had slept together, but he thought he detected a different kind of relationship on show today. Olivia and Vince no longer played zombies. They seemed lively, more forceful, less flunky-like, even though they'd just gushed a stream of flattery – but joking?

Apparently, they'd called at the local newspaper office and

BBC regional headquarters yesterday afternoon to ask journalists familiar with the area whether they detected undercurrents of hate that might at any time produce further local violence. Harpur understood there'd been a mix of responses.

He thought this fairly hopeless research, but Amy might feel they had to justify the cost of their trip somehow. She could write up these visits to the press as very useful, though they would retail only hacks' indecisive guesswork. The minister wouldn't be satisfied with their report, but at least there'd *be* a report. Harpur couldn't see how Ralph would figure in it. Amy's opener today – 'Ember?' – was a mystery. How did it tie in with the Department's tip-off from the Metropolitan Police she'd mentioned?

'We need to go back a little in time,' Olivia said, 'and widen the outlook.' She was about twenty-three or less, mixed-race, Chinese-Brit, small-featured, bright-eyed, slim. She had brown hair worn very short and did some gesticulating, usually in tune with what she said. As far as Harpur could tell, her accent had nothing to do with China. They were around Iles's conference table again. Occasionally she passed her palm over some of its surface in a series of slow semi-circular movements, as though hooked on the feel of wood.

'We're informed that the Met think a décor shop in north London, Kingsbury area, called Jo's And Mil's after the owners, might be a front for some other kind of trade and have it under continuous covert surveillance,' she said. 'Standard observation methods: a first-floor hired room opposite, parked vans and cars on shifts. Unfortunately, they haven't been able to install a bug. Someone's always on the premises. There's a flat.

'Customers can get genuine materials and colour displays, but probably there's additional very private commerce. A garden shack gets some to-ing and fro-ing. The Met don't want their operation compromised so won't disclose what sort of business, but we can speculate, can't we? Drugs wholesaling? Executioner contracts? Money laundering? Thieved jewellery or fine art and antiques disposal? They are very interested in callers at the shop – some of the callers, that is, of course. Obviously, the aim is to break up a network of whatever species it might be and get everyone in it sent down. It's a long-term operation. They insist on keeping control.'

'Are you telling us Ralph was there?' Iles said.

'Olivia is telling you that Ralph Wyverne Ember was there,' Amy said, her voice flat and conclusive, killing off in advance any possible argument. 'It's why I made a question of his name: what was his purpose?'

'But identification?' Iles said. 'How could there be identification?' Harpur knew the ACC would do and say whatever he could to stop this cocky trio from getting ahead of him. He'd find this notion preposterous, especially on his home ground. Aheadness he loved.

'Ralph had an early part of his career in London,' Harpur said. 'He might have been recognized. It was a long time ago, though. Seems unlikely.'

'Detectives shop-watching tail some customers when they leave. Police want to smash the whole set-up,' Olivia said. 'There's the shop and there's the shop's special contacts. These are needed for the eventual prosecution file. It's all slightly random, though. They can't gumshoe every customer. They pick possibles. Ember has a notably scarred face, I gather. It suggested to the officer in charge that this customer might have a shady background, so was worth sticking with for a time.'

Vince read from a notepad. 'The email says the police used one of their routine euphemisms for this figure – "a person of interest".'

'Some reckon Ember stumbled in the kitchen and fell against an open baked-beans can with the lid half up,' Iles said.

Olivia ignored him. 'Ember is tracked and, after a tail-switch, leads to a multi-storey car park where he picks up his vehicle. The distance from the shop apparently helped convince police from the moment he was seen approaching that this customer needed looking into. He didn't park nearer, perhaps, in case his car seemed associated with the shop.'

'Did he know it might be into some sort of villainy?' Iles asked.

'Possibly,' Olivia said. 'The new tail can't follow any further because he or she is on foot, but the police now have the registration number, make and model. Scotland Yard's know-all computer provides the name and address of Ember. His particulars are then fed into another mighty computer which reveals that the Home Office is uncomfortably concerned about a shambles at The Monty club owned by someone of that name, possibly a symptom of general alarming tension over three unsolved murders, those of Raymond Cordovan Street, Clifford Jamieson – known as You-know-who, Paul Favard. The Yard have a word with the Department, give a summary of events, and our duty officer decides it's something Amy is currently involved with and should know about. The encrypted email arrives pre-breakfast. Vince moves in on it immediately.'

'Any message for Amy has to be given priority, regardless of what else I might be engaged with,' Vince said. 'It is an obligation and a pleasure.'

Harpur felt this unction might be another instance of jolly, deliberately overblown banter, but Iles didn't seem to get it. That could happen with him: he expected most people to be unspeakable and so, if they acted unspeakable as a take-off, he didn't see the difference between that and how they really were. He fixed his attention ferociously on Vince and on what Vince had said. For a couple of seconds the ACC looked as if disgust with the last couple of moments might have paralysed him. Once or twice before, Harpur had seen this kind of reaction in Iles when he was affronted by someone's – what he called – 'professional ooze package.' The assistant chief's soul-suffering would be exceptionally severe now because Vince was a code-breaker and should bring light and a true revelation, not the dismal lyrics of a run-of-the-mill bum-suck.

Iles continued to stare at Vince for a time. The paralysis probably prevented adjustments. Harpur thought the ACC must be re-examining in his mind what he would regard as Vince's sick drivel – that is, if Iles's mind wasn't paralysed, too.

But then the ACC began gradually to loosen up. Maybe he'd decided that Vince was covered by one of the assistant chief's favourite maxims, 'Hell is other people,' which he could do in French as well. Vince, tall skinny, middle-aged, long-craniumed, grey-moustached, had to be put up with. He was temporary and so were the other two. They could be short-term tolerated. That's how Iles would see things. He'd soon be back to the areas and realms where he dominated/domineered. 'Ember,' he said, a pronouncement not a query. It sounded like a wipe-out of Amy's shilly-shally with the name.

'You seem almost fond of him,' Amy said.

'He's part of the constituency,' Iles said.

'The Department is not happy with the constituency,' Amy said.

'Oh, dear,' Iles replied.

'This unexplained sojourn of Ember makes us – the Department, that is – uneasy,' Amy said.

'Has the minister a down on paint shops?' Iles said.

'Oh, come on, Mr Iles,' Olivia said.

Harpur thought, yes, Iles did sound pretty feeble. Perhaps he was wearying of the wordage.

'The minister, and several others, wonder why Ember has to travel so far for his paint,' Amy said.

'Unpredictable,' Vince said. 'The word comes up twice in the email from the Department. The minister believes the situation has become more unpredictable because of the paint shop episode.'

'Unpredictability is not a quality the minister is happy with,' Amy said. 'No politician would be happy with it. He feels that for you to go ahead with the Raymond Street function would seriously increase that unpredictability.'

'There are perplexing, worrying links, aren't there,' Olivia said. 'There's Ember, there's the shop and there's you, Mr Iles. Some believe you look after Ralph Ember,' Olivia said. '"Look after" in the sense of . . . in the sense of looking after. There might be a reciprocal element to it. He tries to protect you, perhaps. You possibly know that some in the Department and in the Yard want you suspended while the Paul Favard/ Cliff Jamieson murder investigations are given a restart. We hear of new evidence from Paul's brother, Naunton.'

Iles said: 'I've mentioned, haven't I, that I'm the assistant chief constable (Operations). It's my responsibility to look after, in the sense of . . . well . . . looking after, everyone in my bailiwick. Ask Col.'

'That isn't quite the point,' Amy replied.

'I think it is,' Iles said. 'If you won't ask him, I will,' Iles said. 'Col?'

'Mr Iles has his own way of coming at things,' Harpur replied.

'Which things?' Amy said.

'Issues,' Harpur said.

'Is Raymond Street an issue?'

'Raymond Street's a plaque,' Iles said. 'It's all we have left of him.'

THIRTY

Although The Monty could bring Ralph deep pleasure, therapy and golden hope, the club could also at times cause him terrible anxiety and confusion. Tonight, as he sat at his little desk behind the bar, protected by the *Marriage of Heaven and Hell* floating steel buffer, he had some accounts and invoices to check in front of him, but his mind hankered back to London at the hitman rendezvous.

Tim (Tasteful) Barry-Longville and Mavis, his mother, were at their usual table not far away, and Ralph decided he'd join them in a while with a supply of Cointreau, and Kressmann Armagnac for himself. He remembered feeling ratty with the pair on Bastille Day in the club and he ought to compensate for that. He reckoned they'd been talking against Iles and that had angered him, maybe. Of course, there were metric tonnes to be said against Iles, the vain sod, but Ember couldn't take it from these two. They didn't realize how crucial Iles was to civic well-being and the prime recreational goods market. Ralph didn't want to be harsh on them this evening, though, and expected that he and the drink would do some soothing and smoothing over. In fact Tasteful, wearing one of his glorious custom-made, double-breasted dark suits and a crimson bow-tie, beckoned to him two or three times, as if they had something especially urgent to say. But, for now, Ralph remained with the papers and his nagging thoughts.

He felt troubled about that paint shop visit and the trick he'd pulled at the multi-storey car park. Or tried to pull. It was a bit of very low-level smartness, possibly less. He didn't know anything about surveillance skills and how to block them, except what he'd seen in TV cop dramas. Ember did realize, though, that tails might be switched to avoid detection. This was elementary and obvious to anyone, expert or not.

He'd come out of the café alert to a possible sighting of

the summer jacket and the minor beard, waiting discreetly somewhere for him to reappear. But the summer jacket and minor beard might have signed off his spell and any of twenty people in and around the multi-storey could have taken over. At the swap moment, summer jacket and minor beard might have said to his successor something like: *He's probably aware. He was most likely going for his car but rumbled me and adjusted. He's having a diversionary mug of something in the caff – the usual type dodge.*

Ralph had taken his car, anyway, so the pause had been almost certainly useless – weakly amateur. He should have left by a different door, if the café had one, but this would have needed an explanation to the management. Ralph couldn't face that when he wasn't at all sure there'd been a tail. Summer jacket, minor beard, might have walked on to wherever he was going and done no handover because there was nothing to hand over.

Ralph had taken a quick glance at, say, half a dozen of the women and men nearby in case one of them was obviously eyeballing him. He spotted nobody. But that didn't mean much. Experienced tails would know how to disguise their interest in a target. They'd have been trained to avoid giveaway staring. They'd get seminars in deadpan.

Ralph made himself suppose for five minutes that there *was* definitely a tail, or tails. Who sent him, her, them? Why? These mysteries gave him sharp angst. Police? If so, and if the tail or tails had been with him from the shop to the car park, it must prove, mustn't it, that the shop was under watch and some customers liable to get sticky, slipstream company. Again, why?

Ralph felt it was degrading for a considerable, established businessman to be stalked like this, especially when he was only at the paint shop to safeguard a high-placed police officer, Assistant Chief Constable (Operations) Desmond Iles, by arranging at quite a personal cost for a loud, agitating pest to be put down – put down as humanely as possible, but, in any case, put down.

Who else might want to check Ralph's movements? If the tailing started from the shop, could it be Jo and Mil? What sense did that make, though? He had paid the first-phase money as required and agreed the next steps. They had no reason to doubt him and have him shadowed.

He wondered whether he should do an emergency Sidney Engard Junior call and tell them at the shop that he'd changed his mind absolutely and altogether about the William Morris – had gone off indoor greenery, no longer wanted his stuff, thanks, had come to regard it an unforgivable insult to Nature by sticking a parody of it on urban walls. Although Sidney Engard Senior might favour that style of mock horticulture, his son, Sidney Engard Junior, now fancied a design based on Jackson Pollock.

Being interpreted, this revised order directed at any wire tapper should mean to Mil and Jo that they'd better forget about Naunton Favard, abandon the hit – too many uncertainties. If trouble was on its threatening way to the shop, Ralph feared he might get pulled into it, charged as an accessory to murder.

He was badly mixed up and didn't want to reverse everything by stupid, scampering haste. Ralph was still aware that behind his back some sickeningly disrespectful people called him 'Panicking Ralph', even 'Panicking Ralphy', because of false rumours about dubious incidents in his past. He mustn't give these disgusting slanderers any new evidence to back up that slur.

Yet when the stress really attacked – often since the London visit – he wondered whether his plan to get Waistcoat shot and killed was extreme, was possibly almost absurd. It seemed to Ralph that two motives drove him. Perhaps both were flawed, and seriously flawed. First came The Monty. Waistcoat certainly disgraced the club. The timing made that particularly bad. This was just the period when Ralph believed The Monty's imminent transformation into something much more refined, socially brilliant and intellectually fruitful. A woman felled and injured by a hijacked pool table while carrying drinks was bound to harm the club's image, had possibly destroyed any prospect of advance for years. Naturally, Ralph was infuriated and painfully saddened. He had hoped the drinks were nothing vulgar and cheapo, such as ginger-beer shandy. But wouldn't it be manic to respond to Waistcoat's undoubtedly poor behaviour with slaughter? Excessive? Discourteous? Barbaric? Although the cause might be noble – a reprisal punishment for bringing anarchy to a wonderful local feature, The Monty – there surely had to be proportion. Ralph regarded himself as a great fan of proportion when proportion seemed suitable.

And then, as another motivator, there was the scheme to get rid of Naunton Favard permanently so he could no longer endanger Assistant Chief Constable (Operations) Desmond Iles, and therefore also endanger a splendid era of street peace and calm, so essential to profitable, expanding trade in the commodities. Again, there were moments when Ralph thought that to have someone killed because he menaced a certain kind of commerce in the city was perhaps marginally too severe.

The back-and-forth thinking wearied Ralph. Despite all his quibbles, or perhaps because of them, he could not reach a definite, unvarying decision to stop the Waistcoat death crusade. It was late evening and taking a gaze around The Monty bar, he could remind himself, if that were needed, of what the repaired and refurbished club meant to him. It might help return Ralph to his original belief that anyone capable of bringing disrepute upon this marvellous, welcoming haven probably deserved obliteration soonest.

The Monty had its shortcomings, of course it did. Which club didn't? But it was its lovely potential that delighted and thrilled Ralph. He could not forgive anyone who interfered with that potential, as Waistcoat unquestionably had. Ralph left his desk, loaded a tray with some glasses and bottles and went to sit briefly with Mavis Barry-Longville and Tasteful.

She said: 'Ralph, Timmy has some insights for you from his world as an ace newspaperman on *The Scene*.' Tonight, Mavis wore a turquoise high-necked blouse and a cream-coloured long skirt.

'We had visitors, Ralph,' Tasteful said. 'Government people. A small party – three of them – assertive, persistent, looking for insider stuff on the situation. They'd been to the BBC newsroom as well.'

'Which situation?' Ralph said.

'Well, the situation,' Mavis said.

'Tensions,' Tasteful said.

'Which?' Ralph said.

'Oh, you know, Ralph,' Mavis replied.

On the other side of the room a party was under way to celebrate the early release of two Monty members due to chronic jail overcrowding.

'Home Office trio,' Tasteful said. 'On a quest. A principal, her assistant and a communications guru. This is serious stuff, Ralph.'

'Like in the French Revo,' Mavis said. 'Deputies on Mission, out in the country from Paris to make sure things were going as Mr Robespierre ordered. There's big worry behind these three. Tim says your name was mentioned.'

'Because of here, as a matter of fact,' Tasteful said.

'Here?' Ralph said, but knowing what 'here' meant.

'The Monty, and the bother a while back. The minister has heard of it. He and colleagues grow anxious. So, they dispatch this gifted crew to explore for fear of a repeat, or something bigger and worse.'

'It's to do with Iles, isn't it?' Mavis said.

'Is it?' Ralph said.

'Ultimately, all of it's to do with Iles,' Mavis replied.

'There was a very limited incident at The Monty,' Ralph said. 'It has all been put right as you can see.'

'Commendable,' Mavis snarled. 'Superficial.'

'A fear of serious unrest,' Tasteful said.

'Why, I say think Iles,' Mavis said. 'Three deaths. Who caused them? That's what the "incident" was about.'

'It was a drunken, contemptible few minutes, wholly untypical and unworthy of the club,' Ralph said.

'Definitely untypical,' Mavis said, 'because it concerns an assistant chief. Not the kind of thing that often comes up in a police force.'

The Welcome Home party for the two ex-prisoners had turned to song – 'Goldfinger'. Ralph realized he would miss these sorts of jubilant, raucous get-togethers when he had brought about the big change in The Monty's social rank and rating. Regrettably, they wouldn't fit in tone-wise with Ralph's cherished idea of how the club must be then.

Tasteful said: 'The focus for the moment is on one issue, isn't it?'

'Is it? What?' Ralph replied.

'Halo parade. Should the commem for Raymond Street go ahead, as it normally does every year, or is this likely to touch off more bad trouble?' Tasteful said. 'That's what the visitors want to find out. That's what the Government wants to find out. They were careful about what they said, but I got the idea that suspension of Iles and an independent inquiry is very possible.'

'And what will happen to him after that?' Mavis said. 'Are we talking criminal trial?'

Once again, Ralph had listened to enough. Mavis was probably right, which made Ralph's resolve to get away from her stronger. It wasn't that he had a fierce admiration of Iles and could not bear to hear him knocked. But somehow Iles held things together in this city, and to do it he had to be kept in place. Mavis spoke with a kind of relish about Iles possibly getting put on trial. To Ralph that sounded stupidly short-sighted and evil.

As on Bastille Day, he left the Cointreau bottle, and put the Kressmann back on the bar. He went over to the prisoner release session. Looking ahead once more, Ralph knew he might have trouble deciding if the two liberty lads at the centre of things tonight – Cedric Q. Gowan and Ed-Martin Pone – could have their membership renewed in the transformed Monty. Distressing. Cruel. Inevitable. Of course, they might be inside again, anyway, so there'd be no embarrassment. Cedric and Ed-Martin were great in some aspects, but they wouldn't be comfortable in this altered ambience.

As a matter of fact, Ed-Martin Pone had been serving seven years for a disastrously botched hitman job. These things could go very wrong, especially when so many novices wanted a try, and to get a handgun now was easy.

Thank God, Mil was experienced, though; famed for his ability to put two rounds into a properly nominated chest so accurately that they created what seemed at first a single wound. Ed-Martin Pone's ability had clearly not been at that level. Ralph felt Pone wasn't necessarily a bleak lesson for him about hitmen and hits. No, not necessarily.

Ed-Martin came out from the cheery, singing group – 'Stormy Weather' now, glass in his left hand, and shook Ralph's with his right. 'Grand to see you, Ed,' Ralph said. The handshake was strong and went on for a very hearty while. Ralph tried to work out which of the fingers in his had made a balls-up of the hit, not like one of Mil's.

Ralph wondered occasionally what hitmen's mothers thought of the career they'd chosen. These mothers might have put a lot of energy and time into teaching their son or daughter the basics of civilized living, such as no loud belching and so on, yet the son or daughter still picked a livelihood that completely ignored the demands of civilized existence. In fact, ran counter to them. Perhaps the mothers would argue that their child was only in the hit game part time, but that didn't seem to Ralph a very convincing get-out.

THIRTY-ONE

Harpur easily found the Kingsbury paint shop. A red-letters-on-white board over the door gave the name: Jo's And Mil's. The difficult and essential part would be not to get observed observing. He assumed Olivia had it right and the shop was under non-stop surveillance. And he also assumed the surveillance remained in place.

This was the London borough of Brent, Metropolitan Police territory. Harpur was an outsider, an intruder. Kingsbury had a history going back to the Bronze Age. Later, its name meant 'The King's Manor'. It was not Harpur's manor. Strict protocols existed for an officer operating on ground not his own, and Harpur flouted it, of course. He'd felt compelled to take a look at the shop mentioned by Olivia and the Departmental email – mentioned but not explained. Would this sly trip explain? Maybe not, but he felt he must try. Harpur was like that. He needed to see the actual, not just hear about it: a detective's core response to a mystery.

And plenty of mystery gnawed at him. He could understand how Ralph Ember's Monty and its recent violent troubles might be linked to the dark, pervasive rumours about Iles, but that didn't account for Ralph's London journey and the call on Jo's And Mil's. Harpur thought he did see – half see – one possibility. It was well known that several major London drugs firms wanted to expand and were brutally, often bloodily, extending into provincial towns. Suppose the paint shop was under watch as a front for a big London drugs business, might Ralph want to fix a deal? Was he thinking ahead? Was he pre-empting, or attempting to?

Ralph had quite a brain. He probably didn't know, though, that the paint shop was on the end of top-quality spying. For safety's sake, and to avoid warfare back home, did he hope to create in good time a tidy alliance with one of those powerful, ruthless, colonizing London outfits? He might see this as urgent, in case Assistant Chief Constable (Operations) Iles was removed – suspended, or sacked, and/or jailed. If there was a gap where Iles used to be, one of these London gangs might decide to fill it. Did Ralph want to establish good relations with this potential newcomer? Although Harpur realized that gazing at the outside of the shop like a twerp would probably bring no answer to this, it might be the absolute limit of what he could do. But he'd made the journey, anyway.

Olivia had said the snoop was carried out from a hired room opposite the shop or from a vehicle – car or van – frequently changed. Harpur must stay out of range, but with a reasonable sight of the shop and the shoppers. He thought the same multi-storey car park Olivia had spoken of would just about do. It was a fair distance from the shop, and on the opposite side of the road, but with nothing to block the view.

The building had no windows but low barriers to prevent vehicles overshooting and plunging out, and he took a parking place that let him see over the barrier to the shop from behind his windscreen. Because of CCTV he wouldn't be able to keep this up for very long: a motorist who didn't quit his car could be waiting for a chance to do break-ins. But it would be the same if he'd tried to stay unnoticed in the porch of a neighbouring shop to Jo's And Mil's. Either ploy would draw suspicion and perhaps cause a confrontation. He had to avoid that.

The paint shop seemed to be popular. At first Harpur could see nothing unusual about the steady flow of customers in and out. Some would be householders, others tradesmen needing supplies. Nobody looked to Harpur like a pusher or a baron. Then, though, he focused on a man in dungarees and navy bobble hat apparently making for the shop. There seemed to be a sort of mad bonhomie about him. On his left shoulder the man carried a short, metal, extendable ladder. He might have been a decorator about to pick up some essentials for a job. Yes, he might have been, but probably wasn't.

Iles? Harpur couldn't be certain at once, but got out of the car and went to look up the road directly over the barrier, closer by the length of the Volvo's bonnet. Harpur thought the ACC might be whistling, though the distance even now was too great to be sure his lips were pursed. He walked briskly, holding the ladder with one hand, swinging the other with fine jauntiness. Someone gloriously happy in his career as a decorator and eager to get on with freshening up a room or stairwell today would probably walk like this.

And so did Iles, walk like it in crafty imitation. 'Whistle while you work' – was that the assistant chief's aggressively cheery warble now? Anyone seeing this man for the first time would unquestionably believe he was good with wallpaper, never mismatching patterns. Taking obvious care not to clock anyone with the ladder, he went into the shop. Normally, Iles wouldn't have minded hitting people with a ladder or with anything else that could assert superiority but avoid the tedium of words. He was into theatricals now, though, and his chosen role demanded a sweet show of caring and harmlessness. When he came out ten minutes later he was carrying in his free hand what Harpur could see was a pot of paint. Iles's left still held the ladder.

Had he done the same analysis of the situation as Harpur's own? Did the ACC see similar risky likelihoods of additional, unwanted drugs business on his ground? Iles had created an unspoken but binding arrangement with Ralph and Mansel Shale that provided toleration of their businesses in exchange for guaranteed peace on the streets. A London invader could disrupt and possibly destroy that neat, civilized treaty. And so, like Harpur, Iles would want to know what Ralph Ember was doing with a possible big, big-city drugs syndicate.

When he left the shop, Iles turned towards the multi-storey. This surprised Harpur. He would have expected the ACC to take the ladder and pot of paint back to wherever he had parked. Unextended, the ladder would fit into the cabin of a saloon car. Naturally, if he was a genuine decorator, the shop might have been on his way to the job and he could call in en route for the pot of paint required. But he wasn't a decorator; he was Assistant Chief Constable (Operations) Desmond Iles.

In a little while, Harpur saw why he'd been wrong to assume the ACC would go back the way he had just come. He looked up at the enormous frontage of the multi-storey and focused instantly on Harpur standing at the barrier. Iles gave a kind of imperfect wave with the pot-of-paint hand. There could be no finger flexibility in the wave because the assistant chief's fingers had to clasp the pot. In fact, the wave didn't really look like a wave, more like someone shaking a lemonade bottle to get the bubbles gallivanting. Iles's left still held the ladder in a steadying grip on his shoulder.

Harpur waved back. It seemed the decent thing to do. Obviously, he found it a pain that Iles picked him out like that from such a huge background, but the ACC couldn't help being so fucking smart. Harpur recognized that he should have grown used to the assistant chief's blazing all-round talents by now. Occasionally, Iles would speak about his mother, and made her sound effortlessly malign and vindictive. Perhaps this had made Iles brilliantly clever to crush her.

Harpur got back into his car. After a few minutes, Iles opened the passenger door and joined him. Because of the ladder he'd been forced to use the stairs not the lift. He leant the ladder against the barrier with the paint pot underneath. He took off the bobble hat and put it into the pocket of his dungarees.

'My own view, do you want it, Col?' the ACC said.

'Why not, sir?' Harpur replied.

'First, that the two people running the shop don't know they're being watched; and second, that they would be capable of all sorts, on top of the commodities game.'

'Which all sorts?'

'All sorts. They'd take on anything.'

Harpur wondered whether he was seeing the difference between himself and the ACC. If Iles wanted to know something about a shop and its people and its customers, he'd go in and try to find it, whereas Harpur hung back, alert but passive behind a barrier, hoping that something significant would happen and that he would spot it. Iles behaved as if the world was in debt to him, and he'd collect whenever he wanted to.

'There's a kind of exuberant devilishness about Jo and Mil,' Iles said.

'You think they have form?'

'Possibly they've got away with it so far,' Iles said.

'Did you pick up a tail after the shop?' Harpur replied.

'Tail?'

'As possibly being more than what you seem.'

'My whole life is like that, Harpur. It's a kind of economizing. I try to lease out only segments of myself. I'm no spendthrift with my selfhood. I keep reserves. I might need them.'

'Quite a few would be intrigued to hear this,' Harpur said.

'Which?'

'Which what, sir?'

'Which few?'

'Quite a few.'

'You?'

'Shall I give you a lift with the gear to where you're parked?' Harpur asked.

'The Jo element of that business, or those businesses, is a very comely piece,' Iles said.

'Does she go for artisans?'

THIRTY-TWO

Although there were certainly times when Harpur regretted having his name, address and phone number in the directories, on the whole he regarded it as not only a useful thing to do but a proper thing to do. If people needed help, they ought to know where and how they could get it. Of course, some would argue that anyone needing help should dial the 999 emergency number and get police or fire brigade or ambulance or all of them. But not everybody wanted that kind of official public aid. Iles's wife, Sarah, for instance, would not like to turn to any of these services, but she hadn't minded calling the other day at Harpur's house with her worries.

And now there was Melanie Younger: small, pretty, slight, agitated, plaintive; the one-time girlfriend, possible fiancée, of Raymond Street. It was early evening. As often happened if someone came without pre-arrangement, Harpur was at work, and for a while his daughters had to do the hosting. When he arrived today, Hazel, Jill and the guest were in the sitting room with cups of tea and biscuits.

Harpur sat down on the chesterfield. Hazel poured him some tea. 'We've had a good talk, Dad,' she said.

Oh, God.

'This is in some ways a very sad visit, but in another way it's lovely, Dad,' Jill said. 'If you ask "Why sad?", Dad, I would reply, "Because it is to do with a death." If you ask, "Why lovely?" I would answer, "Because Melanie is to be wed."'

'Yes? Oh, many congratulations, Melanie,' Harpur said.

'The man she loved first is dead,' Jill said. 'He is that death I mentioned. But it doesn't mean because he is dead she can't later on love someone else and want to marry him. It would be such a waste to be in love only with someone who's dead.'

'Yes,' Harpur replied.

'That would make death a winner, and turn mourning into a career,' Jill said. 'Bad, bad, bad.'

'Right,' Harpur said.

'There's a poem we did at school that says death shouldn't be proud because it's not so mighty and dreadful as it thinks,' Hazel said, 'and all the best people do it – die.'

'For instance, you loved Mum, Dad, but now she's dead and you've got Denise instead,' Jill said.

'Right,' Harpur said.

'Although she's only twenty that doesn't matter,' Jill said.

'No,' Harpur said.

'She smokes a lot but one day she might give it up,' Jill said. 'If she gets a cough she would know she'd better stop, owing to her undoubted lungs.'

'Yes,' Harpur said.

'You can still love her,' Jill said.

'Yes,' Harpur said.

'And she's brainy, knowing French et cetera, so being only twenty doesn't really come into it.'

'No,' Harpur said.

'Think of that composer, Mozart,' Jill said.

'Right,' Harpur said.

'Mozart was only a kid when he wrote some great symphonies.'

'Yes,' Harpur replied.

'But it's not exactly the same with Melanie,' Jill said.

'Not the same as Mozart?' Harpur said.

'Not quite. Melanie needs a bridge,' Jill said.

'A bridge?' Harpur said.

'Kind of,' Jill said.

'Between what and where?' Hazel asked.

'Plus what are known as plaques come into it. This is why I said about a bridge,' Jill replied.

'Right,' Harpur said.

'You've met Melanie before, haven't you, Dad, at the time of the death,' Jill said.

'Yes,' Harpur said.

'Those were terrible times, Mr Harpur,' Melanie said. She

had on a navy tracksuit and red and white training shoes. Her
hair was pulled back into a bun on the back of her neck.

'Yes, terrible,' Harpur said.

'Melanie is scared in case there is a return to them days,'
Jill said.

'"Those",' Harpur said.

'Those what?' Jill said.

'"Those days",' Harpur said. 'Not "them".'

'That's what I said – not them days again,' Jill said.

'OK,' Harpur said.

'She used to snort,' Jill said.

'Yes,' Harpur said.

'Stress,' Jill replied.

'Yes,' Harpur said. He thought there might have been a short
time when Melanie went on the game to finance her snorts.
No need to mention that now.

'The plaque is to do with them days,' Jill said. 'That's the thing
with plaques – they are about the past. They are in the present
because they are fixed on a wall where people can see them
now, but they are not *about* now but about the past. They are
to remind people what happened in a previous time. Hazel
spoke about a poet. If a poet, years back, lived in a certain
house, they would put a plaque on it to say this had been his
place. That would be a really nice plaque and helpful if a
scholar wanted to know where the poet lived and wrote his
or her poems with a big feather sharpened at one end so it
became a pen. If the scholar asked for directions, someone
might answer, "You can't miss it because there's a plaque." If
the poet could come back from the dead and see the plaque
on his or her house, it would give him or her a true joy and
make all the poems he or she had done seem worthwhile. He
or she would go off if he or she was a ghost and write another
poem about it all. There are plenty of rhymes for "plaque".'

'Right,' Harpur said.

'But some plaques are about really awful things. This is
why I said sad,' Jill replied.

'So when's the happy date, Melanie?' Harpur asked.

'She doesn't want anything to sort of mess things up,'
Jill said. 'Such as to do with a plaque.'

'Melanie has heard rumours, strong rumours,' Hazel said.

'Well, I suppose we all have.'

'Trouble,' Jill said.

'Possible trouble – fresh trouble,' Hazel said, 'like that roughhouse at The Monty, and maybe worse.'

'I'll try to explain it for you,' Jill said.

'Oh, thanks,' Hazel said.

'No need to be snotty-sarky,' Jill said.

'Isn't there?' Hazel said.

'Haze doesn't want to get deep about it all, Melanie, because there was something very special going on between her and Desy Iles.'

'That's enough, Dandruff Queen,' Hazel said.

'It's over now, but she's still a bit touchy about it,' Jill replied. 'The bridge – she wouldn't want to talk about the bridge. But the bridge is what Melanie needs, isn't it, Melanie? You'd like a bridge to Des Iles, wouldn't you? Dad, I think Melanie hopes you'll speak to him for her, you being so close to him at work. That's why she's here.'

'It's the Ray Street plaque at police headquarters,' Melanie said.

'There's a plaque about him because he was murdered when he was undercover,' Jill said.

'Dad knows this, you idiot,' Hazel said.

'That plaque could get some hates going,' Jill said. 'Melanie doesn't want big aggro around about one boyfriend when she's going to marry another one. This could really upset the new fiancé. He could get quite jealous of the dead one and the plaque can bring out all sorts of stuff about the past which might not be good for a marriage.'

'I'd like Mr Iles to stop the halo parade anniversary event for Ray this year,' Melanie said. 'Some people think too much fuss is made about Ray and not enough about the other two deaths.'

'And so there's envy and anger,' Hazel said.

Jill said: 'Some believe Des Iles doesn't want the two murders case solved because he—'

'Shut it, bitch,' Hazel replied.

'There's such a thing as vengeance,' Jill said. 'Someone is

dead, such as Raymond Street, and the court couldn't find who did it. So someone else might decide to take over and double it.'

'Illegal,' Hazel said.

'Of course,' Jill replied.

THIRTY-THREE

The death of Waistcoat in that terrible fashion came as a bit of a shock to Ralph. OK, admittedly he'd contracted Mil Parvin for the hit, and had already paid half a respectable fee to juice things nicely along, but Ralph lately began to wonder whether it might be an over-extreme measure, and was wondering about further discussion. He'd often heard or seen that phrase, 'further discussions', on TV news or in the press when some major political row was under way, and he liked the impression it gave of decent orderliness and patience. This, surely, was a worthwhile objective.

Second thoughts like this did sometimes take hold of Ralph. He knew that some would call it indecisiveness, even jitteriness. No, not at all, but a sign of disciplined thinking or re-thinking, free from the pressures of that earlier, possibly hasty, decision. Only fools never changed their minds.

He could still see the logic that had made him feel Naunton (Waistcoat) Favard must be removed, and soon. It was entirely reasonable to fear that Waistcoat would go on making dangerous trouble unless he was stopped, and the only way he could be finally and permanently stopped was to have him seen off. Ralph had handed over totally honest instalment money to have that done, and he would cough up the rest when unquestionably due.

But he had come to wonder whether something less could work with Waistcoat. For instance, he might be given a blunt, unencrypted warning. Or he could get very thoroughly beaten up but just not to the point of death, and breakages confined to the limbs, nothing extravagant. Someone left in that state would most likely not invite more of it by rudely bellyaching again about the Paul Favard and You-know-who deaths. After a suitable period of recovery Waistcoat, given that kind of corrective, should be able to get back to almost a normal life with pain well under control.

Obviously, Mil would no longer be entitled to the full Rest In Peace fee if one of these changes to the original commission was picked. He'd already received half and Ralph would not have attempted to get any of it back if the situation had been perfectly and sweetly resolved by a good and very serious chin-wagging and/or hammering.

Ralph accepted that if he took part in this kind of operation he might have to put up with some sizeable losses. That's what business was about: risk, chancing, possible reversal, a start again elsewhere. But, plainly, if the killing had been called off, Ralph would not have paid the remaining half of the original agreed fee, but that could be dealt with in civilized, sensible talks that took account of radically altered circumstances. Ralph might have agreed to a small, goodwill, token amount, instead of the full second contribution.

Now, though, there had been total completion of the Waistcoat project and the stated remainder of the payment would definitely be due. Ralph's uneasiness about it all did continue for a while, but he wholeheartedly accepted that a contract was a contract, whether written or only spoken, and its terms had to be followed, or what would happen to standard commercial life? That standard did not come automatically. It had to be actively preserved. Appalling chaos threatened otherwise. Ralph never stopped worrying about chaos.

The news of the death was not official yet. Ralph heard of it in two separate, but more or less identical versions, from members of The Monty. Ralph would have been sceptical about the tip-off if there were only one. But the fact that the information came from two people, and with details that were consistent, more or less convinced Ralph of their truth. Ralph did recognize that, although the information had two sources, what those two sources delivered might have reached them from only one source. Ralph doubted that, though.

And, of course, in a way the news was only to be expected, and consequently more credible. There had been an agreement between Ralph and Mil Parvin to finish Waistcoat, and it appeared now that he had been eliminated. Rest In Perpetuity. Ralph remembered from school that if you solved a problem in maths you could write at the end, 'QED', Latin for 'Which was to be demonstrated.' Ralph thought that with a couple of slight changes this could be applied here about Waistcoat: who was to be destroyed. But perhaps that was a flippant way of looking at the situation. Ralph certainly did not feel flippant. He felt burdened, weighed down by the need to pay up for something he wasn't sure he believed in any longer. 'Irrelevant, Ralph; footling, Ralph,' he told himself. 'There was a binding commitment. It's still binding, only more so, because the purpose of the commitment has been committed.'

In what Ralph recognized as a weird way, it really pissed him off that these sources of the news obviously never supposed he might have done the job on Waistcoat Favard himself. Neither of them started their report with something like, 'As you might know, Ralph,' or 'Waistcoat deserved it, didn't he, Ralph? Bravo!', or when they were talking to others, 'Ember had enough motive, for God's sake, didn't he? Waistcoat had undoubtedly brought violence, destruction, terror to The Monty, at a time when Ralph was ardently trying to fashion a new dignified image for the club in the style of, say, The Athenaeum.'

Those two who had come to Ralph with the news would not know about such ambitions, but they would certainly know he loved The Monty, and yet did not go after the vandal who tried to wreck it. Did that pair think Ralph was too weak and timorous to see to Waistcoat, and punish him for his foul behaviour? Did they think Ralph was afraid of being attacked by a pool table?

They probably knew that filthy nickname some gave Ember, 'Panicking Ralph'. Did they regard it as accurate and justified? Perhaps they each assumed that Ralph didn't already know at first hand – Ralph's own – everything about the death because he'd be too yellow himself to make such a revenge attack. Instead, he needed to be briefed on the quiet about it by those who did know at least the central truth: Waistcoat was dead.

'And the defacement,' Tommy Whale said. He'd been the first to speak to Ralph. 'So unnecessary, so disgracefully extra. The slaughter might be all very well, a run-of-the-mill kill, but restructuring of features is surely excessive, like delight in butchery.'

'To take time to do all that. It's macabre,' Basil (Notable) Maltby said. He'd joined Ralph and Tommy.

'The funeral will be useful,' Whale said. 'We should obviously attend to confirm he's really a goner. He did his rotten best to drag the club down, so we need to show who won that contest. It will be worth dressing up for. I don't think I've ever been to a funeral of someone whose face has been realigned. It wouldn't be visible, of course. There won't be a lying-in-state for Waistcoat Favard. But gossip about something like that gets around, especially if we help, and people will be conscious of it.'

Although in some ways the speed at which things had moved scared and wrong-footed Ralph, he also suddenly felt very powerful and formidable. He had given instructions for the elimination of a pest and that pest had been more or less immediately seen off – no dithering, no funking, when it came to the actual cheerio. Ralph W. Ember had spoken, and when he spoke someone responded at once with the required action.

As it appeared to Ralph, Mil was probably afraid of him, and knew that once the agreement was finalized he had better carry out what Ralph required. Ralph was someone who stipulated jobs to be done and he expected them to be done immediately. Ralph could sympathize. Mil was not much more than a kid. He would be very aware that he was dealing with someone – Ralph – who had seen and successfully taken an elegant part in so much of business life, and who was also famed for important thinking about the environment, rivers particularly. Mil was bound to experience a degree of awe.

Virtually all Ralph's drugs income was cash, and he always had plenty in safes at home and in his Monty office, though most of his outgoings – to suppliers – were cash, too, and cash on a much plumper scale than what he would be handing over to Mil now. He took £20,000 again from one of The Monty safes and distributed the notes around four or five pockets, as he usually did when carrying an amount of currency.

He deliberately drew more than the agreement required. He didn't want Mil to think the payment came from some special designated treasure house. He'd like it to look as though he always had a decent sum aboard as part of normal string-along living; like, say, for paying taxi fares and/or a girl, and he'd make it obvious that having filtered off Mil's share, Ralph wouldn't be short. Of course he wouldn't. Outgoings of this kind weren't negligible, but they were absolutely no strain, either. He wasn't like a kid emptying the piggy bank. And because the agreement had now definitely come into force, he didn't have to worry that Jo might increase the demand: he'd made a payment.

The contract – verbal – said this second payment should be made within forty-eight hours of the death's official confirmation. Ralph didn't feel certain that words from Tommy Whale and Notable amounted to official statements, but they were two Monty stalwarts he knew well, and he felt they wouldn't lie about something so meaty. They named no place and no date or time in their news and this did trouble Ralph. It might restart his fears that Tommy and Notable had a common tipster who gave and withheld the same bits of information. Ralph pressed for more detail but they had none, or said they had none. He had to choose, accept what they said, or not.

He decided to accept. Even if they had things wrong, there'd be no great damage. Ralph would call at the Kingsbury paint shop and hear the truth from Mil himself. He might say, 'Yes', it had been done, in which case Ralph would reply, 'Thank you very much', pass the money over and go home. If he said, 'Not yet', Ralph would let him feel he should finish the assignment soon and he'd hang on to the money until he made the next visit, which should not be delayed.

He drove to Kingsbury and parked again in the multi-storey. He'd seen no signs that he'd been tracked there last time, so felt reasonably sure he had no company. This easiness of mind left him, though, almost as soon as he entered the shop. Conditions had massively changed. Mil blared a greeting, to Mr Engard, asked at maximum voice about Ralph's decorating plans, and said they should discuss the refurbishment scheme at leisure out in the yard where they wouldn't be interrupted.

And he did mean the yard, rather than the sort of outhouse-studio where they had spoken last time. There was a strip of grass alongside this small building with a rustic bench on it.

Mil brought a brochure of some sort with him and they sat
down. He spread a couple pages of the brochure on the bench
between them. Smiling sweetly, he pointed at an array of
variously coloured front doors, giving Ember – Engard Junior
– Ralph a range of choices. 'There've been disastrous developments, Ralph,' he said.

'Which?'

'We're scared of bugging of the inside areas,' Mil said. He
kept his head low as he talked. Ralph thought this could
be to defeat lip-readers. 'We found yesterday that they've got
us under continuous scrutiny. They watch us here and are
with us wherever we go.'

'My God,' Ralph said.

'Phone tap as well,' Mil said. 'Well, we've always been a
bit anxious about the phone – why we invented Sidney Engard
Junior, with his affection for William Morris. It was Jo who
noticed symptoms of interference on the line lately.'

'So how the hell did you do it?'

'Do what?'

'The job.'

'Which?'

'Waistcoat Favard, what else?' Ralph said.

'What about him?'

'Done.'

'Done?'

'Taken out,' Ralph said.

'Killed?'

'And carved.'

'Oh, thanks, Ralph.'

'Thanks?'

'Someone cuts him about so you think it must be me.'

'Not you?' Ralph replied.

'Like you said, how could it be? I've got a non-stop shadow.'

'I brought the money.' Ember realized he sounded idiotic
and feeble. His hopes for something with Jo had just sunk.

'That's gorgeous of you, but you'll have to take it home. I
can't risk being seen accepting great lumps of cash from you,
even if you wanted to pay for nothing, as it would be. Go
carefully. You might get a shadow yourself.'

THIRTY-FOUR

les had one of his chuckles. These were fairly rare and usually had little to do with humour. They seemed sincere, though, and generally signified a victory he'd brought off against someone – or more than one – who'd disgustingly shown dangerous but foolish enmity towards him. If you looked hard and had some minutes available, you might detect an element of pity in the sound rolling out from him, as though he always disliked being so brilliantly right and could sympathize with those he so effortlessly destroyed.

'I believe quite a few thought I'd done it, Col,' Iles said. 'They believed – honestly believed – they saw an obvious motive. Very obvious. After all, Waistcoat Favard was campaigning to get a case against me brisked up, revitalized, and not a trivial case – not at all: a double murder case. I mean the You-know-who and Paul Favard deaths in not very charming circumstance. Didn't they try to bring suspicion on me by creating that foul disturbance at dear Ralphy's beloved club? And Waistcoat had some apparent success. So we got those three devoted stirrers from the Home Office – Amy et cetera – asking rough questions wherever the breeze took them. Vindictive, Col. All built on slander, Col. Dirty warfare, Col.'

'Chief Inspector Francis Garland is investigating the Naunton Favard murder, sir,' Harpur said.

'Of course he is. Francis is a very talented officer.'

'Certainly.'

'He knows he mustn't give any weight to these absurd, evil rumours about myself. They are bound to lead to fret and floundering. Top legal brains at the Home Office have now decided that any further moves against me would be oppressive and malicious. Such investigation on any front is now officially deemed to be not in the public interest.'

'I think the public would be *very* interested,' Harpur said.

A postscript chuckle came from Iles. They were talking in

Harpur's suite at headquarters, Iles moving about in full glossy gear for some formal civic luncheon he had to attend later. He still received invitations to these functions, despite having occasionally given huge offence by his words and behaviour at similar gatherings. Organizers must fear that if they dropped him he'd come anyway and cause even more thorough distress.

Iles said: 'I'm Operations, so naturally Francis keeps me informed, and this does seem a tricky one, Colin. Such reprehensible extras.'

'To the face, you mean?' Harpur said.

'Rearrangement. Wilful and unnecessary. Gaudy.'

'True,' Harpur said.

'I'm delighted Nature came to my aid. Could there be a better alibi?' Iles said.

'Hard to think of one, sir,' Harpur said. 'I hope Sarah is well.'

'I being at the birth of my second child and first son,' Iles replied. 'The medics put the death time for Waistcoat at the more or less identical moment as arrival of the baby. I expect you'll see after your dreamy fashion a kind of profound commentary on Life itself, Col – the death of Waistcoat countered, as it were, by the delivery of Leopold Helicon to Sarah: a well-warranted death gloriously upstaged by a splendid new child. It has a virtually religious flavour, doesn't it – sin, salvation?'

'Great, sir,' Harpur said.

'And you, definitely not present at the birth or the conception, Harpur. I expect in your small-minded, mischievous way you'd like to remind me I had the snip. In turn, Harpur, I would remind you that I also had the reconnect.'

'Grand, sir.'

THIRTY-FIVE

Iles decided that the commemorative ceremony marking the anniversary of Ray Street's death could go ahead as usual. The assistant chief used a number of ways to help offset his pain and self-blame for sending Street on that catastrophic mission. This was one. Harpur knew Iles could never reconcile himself fully to that loss, though. His grief wasn't specific to Street. It would have been the same for anyone – anyone he had responsibility for. Sentimental? A leadership flaw? Softness? He could be disabled now and then by memory of a death. Perhaps the halo parade occasions affected everyone like that, but Iles more than others. His obvious vulnerability might be why he stayed stuck at Assssissstant. Yes, Ssssoftnesssss.

Melanie Younger, Street's one-time girlfriend, didn't turn up for the Street ceremony. 'Regrettable,' Iles said, 'understandable. She looks to the future. She has a fiancé to appease. We also look to the future, and draw strength to help us from our past.'

Mansel Shale did show. He had on a fine three-piece suit, a crimson, large-winged bow-tie, and a folded azure silk handkerchief billowing out of his top pocket. Harpur could tell care had gone into choice of this ensemble, the aim deep respect. That handkerchief was an adornment, a tribute. No snot would get blown into it.

Harpur thought this was the first time Shale had ever attended one of the anniversary functions. He had come through a lot of grief and suffering, but seemed stronger and more positive today than Harpur had noticed for months – ebullient, almost. Some particular achievement or victory appeared to have restored his old confidence and spirit. It was as if not just this local triumph, whatever it might be, had made things close by looking rosier, but he seemed to radiate a worldwide delight in all of life wherever.

'Manse!' Harpur said when the meeting broke up. 'Lovely to see you.'

'Thank you, Mr Harpur.' Shale's voice had a touch of heartiness and grandeur.

'You look well.'

'Things have been returned to normal.'

'Except that Waistcoat's death remains a mystery,' Harpur said.

'We're used to deaths that remain a mystery, aren't we, Mr Harpur? In some cases it's better like that.'

'Oh?'

'Yes, indeed,' Shale replied, 'much better.'

9 781847 519900